"You can't fall in love with me."

Devon started, then stared at Grey. She could tell he already regretted his impulsive words.

"Nothing will happen," Grey continued harshly. "I'm far too old for you."

"You're not kidding!"

"And too experienced."

"Oh, la-de-da!"

"I know you probably think I cut a fairly romantic figure—"

"I think no such thing."

"—but you can forget any plans you have for seducing me. I'm not interested in vulnerable young women. I'm particularly not interested in a virgin."

"A virgin? Don't tell me *that's* written in my file!"

"Lady, it's written all over you."

Quinn Wilder, a Canadian writer, was born and raised in Calgary, but now lives in the Okanagan Valley away from the bustle of a city. She has had a variety of jobs, but her favorite pastime has always been writing. She graduated from the Southern Alberta Institute of Technology Journalism Arts program in 1979. Since then, she has free-lanced, and her list of credits includes magazine articles, educational material, scripts and speeches. Her first novel became a Harlequin Romance, marking a high point in her career. She enjoys skiing and horseback riding.

Books by Quinn Wilder

HARLEQUIN ROMANCE

2772—THAT MAN FROM TEXAS
2886—TO TAME A WILD HEART
2904—DAUGHTER OF THE STARS
3096—HIGH HEAVEN
3191—OUTLAW HEART
3258—RIDE A STORM

DEVON'S DESIRE
Quinn Wilder

Harlequin Books

TORONTO • NEW YORK • LONDON
AMSTERDAM • PARIS • SYDNEY • HAMBURG
STOCKHOLM • ATHENS • TOKYO • MILAN
MADRID • WARSAW • BUDAPEST • AUCKLAND

Original hardcover edition published in 1991
by Mills & Boon Limited

ISBN 0-373-03273-0

Harlequin Romance first edition July 1993

DEVON'S DESIRE

CHAPTER ONE

TROUBLE.

A man like that meant trouble, Devon Paige decided, as she slipped through the open door into the library. He was a tall man, dressed very conservatively in a gray suit that must have been custom-cut to fit over the breadth of his immense shoulders. Expensive suits were common enough here at Redwoods, her father's California estate house, so what was it that had danger warnings dancing up and down her spine?

Though she could have sworn she hadn't made a sound, he had turned the moment she entered the room, and his eyes were resting on her now, intensely and formidably gray, like winter storm clouds boiling up over a frozen horizon. Her uneasiness increased.

"Oh, Devon, there you are!"

She turned her attention briefly to her father, and unconsciously her huge hazel eyes narrowed. Her father was looking cherubic behind his huge desk, rather like a contented Buddha. Which could mean only one thing.

Trouble.

She gave her hair, long and thick and the color of liquid honey, a shake, which made her look defiant and ready for battle. What was he up to now? And what did it have to do with—her gaze slanted back to the other man—this rather terrifyingly masculine specimen?

Something did not ring true about the man. And it was those expensive clothes. They seemed as if they were intended to cloak his raw physical strength in civility, but they failed. Though he had remained motionless since she entered the room, the cut of his muscle, pressed into the line of the superbly fitted clothing, suggested a man of movement, of athletic ability, of pure physical power, that was not at all in keeping with the paunchy types of her father's set. Even her father's more youthful protegés had that office pallor, that fineness of build that suggested desks and fluorescent lights.

This man was bronzed, permanently colored by wind and sunshine, rugged.

His face was as powerful as his build, but not in a way Devon found inviting. There was a schooled impassiveness in his features. He was neither smiling nor frowning, and yet she got the impression of coldness. The impression was underlined by his eyes. They were a perfect match for the nondescript color of his suit, except that the eyes were anything but nondescript. They glittered as cold as ice forming on a mountain stream. And they alone denied the disciplined impassiveness of his stance and his features. The eyes were watchful—hard and cold and watchful.

Devon felt herself taking a steadying breath.

Trouble.

He was not the businessman that the suit, and his neat, short dark brown hair, might suggest. This type of man did not belong in her father's library.

"Devon, this gentleman is from the Government——"

Gentleman? Well, the term had been used loosely for centuries, on everything from gunfighters to riverboat gamblers. But the Government? He wasn't what one pictured a civil servant looking like. Nor did he suit her admittedly Hollywood-inspired image of an IRS agent. And he didn't look nearly glossy enough to be a politician. No, he definitely would have smiled by now if he was a politician.

She slid him another look, to find his eyes already resting on her, his gaze bland and unapologetic.

"He's from the Federal Law Enforcement Agency." Her father said this in a weighty tone that suggested she was supposed to be either impressed or intimidated. Devon decided, rebelliously, to be neither.

"What an unfortunate acronym!" she murmured, and out of the corner of her eye she saw the tall man start, and eye her with a surprised and reluctant appreciation that was quickly masked. She liked surprising people. She marked herself one on her side of the scoreboard, then wondered why she felt an intuitive need to keep score against a man who had yet to speak a word.

Because of the danger hanging in the air, she supposed. She hoped she was wrong, but she could just smell a battle brewing.

"They've come about the letters I've been getting," her father went on.

"Letters?" Buzzers now joined the warning lights that had been going off in her head since she had first come through that door not two minutes ago.

"Ridiculous things—misspelled and grubby. But we're working on some very sensitive Government contracts at the plant right now, particularly the Hart project, and it seems we warrant protection. It appears there's an off chance the letters may be coming from a terrorist organization."

Devon eyed her father narrowly. "*We* warrant protection? Meaning the factory?"

"Actually, meaning us, personally. It seems the terrorists might see you as a way to Hart...er...my soft underbelly, so to speak."

"Oh, for heaven's sake!" spluttered Devon. She eyed her father suspiciously. Was this his latest move in a chess game they'd been playing since she'd declared her independence two years ago, and left home? He hated his lack of control over her life. Hated it. Was he capable of engineering a situation like this so he could keep a closer eye on her? She suspected he was, though she couldn't very well accuse him of that with a law enforcement officer standing right here, and without a shred of evidence against him. Besides, Flint-Eye would probably arrest him in a second if she even hinted at such a thing, and, misguided as her father was, and irritating as his chronic interference in her life tended to be, Devon would have felt terrible if he got himself into real trouble. Even if it did serve him right.

She sighed heavily. He really had gone too far this time. But she should have known something was coming. He'd been all too complacent about her refusal to give him her address after the last humiliation he'd subjected her to.

"I'd like to see the letters," she demanded.

"Oh, I don't think that will be necessary. They're very vulgar."

Devon's suspicion increased.

"Meanwhile, until we get to the bottom of this, you'll be escorted about your daily affairs," her father told her.

Well, there it was. Trouble, in capital letters.

She took a step toward her father, and lowered her voice in a small attempt to be polite to her father's guest.

"If you think for one moment that I am going to have this goon follow me through my daily life, you are sadly, *sadly* mistaken." She slanted the man who flanked her on her right a brief, searching look, but, if her voice had carried, his face remained indifferent to her insult.

"Devon, really——"

"Don't you 'really' me, Father!" She dropped her voice a little lower. "Do you think I'd allow you to checkmate me so easily? I've known you've been hatching something since I moved out of that lovely little brownstone that you made into Fort Knox overnight!"

"It was just for your protection——"

"Steel girds over the windows? A doorman? I intend to live a normal life, and I'm warning you, if you want to be part of it, you'd better let go of your liking for little schemes such as this!"

"This isn't a scheme," her father denied. He was trying, and failing, to conceal his delight in the situation.

"I am going to lead a normal life." Her voice lost its guarded tone altogether.

"You're a Paige! How can a Paige lead a normal life? And look what happened to poor Uncle Charlie."

"Oh, for heaven's sake! You aren't going to haul up that old chestnut again, are you?" Devon demanded.

"Excuse me."

The quiet, steel-threaded voice had an unmistakable note of boredom in it. Devon was somewhat flustered to find the cool gray eyes resting, not on her father's face, but on her own. How dared this aggravating interloper look at her as if she was causing problems, when it should have been so obvious it was her father who was the habitual troublemaker?

"My orders have your name on them, Miss Paige. You can argue with your father for the next three hours if you want to. You can even win. But it's still going to be your name on my orders, and unless my boss changes his mind, which is unlikely, you're stuck with me for a while."

"And that's that, dear." Her father actually had the nerve to chuckle.

Devon wondered blackly if there was an equivalent to the Academy Awards for manipulation. She had to content herself with bestowing her most furious look on him. She severely doubted that a threat serious enough to wipe out her personal freedom had occurred. She was made even more furious by his look of smug pleasure. There was a hair of a possibility he had not engineered the threat—but there was no doubting he was immensely pleased with it, and this new opportunity to keep tabs on his nonconformist daughter. Well, he hadn't won yet.

Devon turned her gaze to the stranger who had just invaded her life, and his impassive features brought her fury to a fresh boil. How dared he stand there looking bored and unmoved by the absolute ruin that was being wrought on the so carefully guarded borders of her private life?

"This is a total waste of the taxpayers' money," she informed him, her tone snapping like flags in a high wind. "My having a personal bodyguard is absolutely and utterly ridiculous!"

She didn't know what she had expected. Some sort of change in those rocky features. Disagreement. Disapproval. Sympathy. *Anything.*

Instead his eyes flicked over her with a flat lack of interest in the emotional upheaval his presence would wreak on her life.

"Yes, ma'am," he agreed politely, and with a brazen lack of conviction.

She hadn't liked him before he spoke, something about him zinging disagreeably across her nerve endings. Now she liked him even less.

She gazed at him haughtily, refusing to look away. A trace of sardonic humor glinted briefly in his eyes.

"Perhaps you'd like to address a complaint to your Congressman."

Her mouth fell open. His tone, save for an almost indiscernible trace of irony, had not changed one iota, as cool and uninterested as though he'd told a parking lot attendant to bring him his car.

Her dislike intensified into something that approached hate. The nerve of the man! For a moment she had the astounding urge to childishly stamp her foot, but she quelled it and lifted her chin. She flung her head at her father, turned on her heel and marched out. She was far from surrender, though she had definitely lost round one.

"Come along, then," she ordered Flint-Eye coldly. Snapping at him gave her some small illusion of face-saving control. It also gave her the satisfaction of seeing a grim tightening of those firm lips, and a flash of fire in the cool gray of those eyes. So he wasn't rock all the way through to his heart, she surmised. Just most of the way.

In the hall, a strong hand locked on her shoulders, and she found herself spun around. She felt shocked both by his audacity and by the electric jolt that reverberated down her arm. She tilted her chin upward in defiance of his menacing expression.

"Don't touch me!" She directed her most wilting look at him.

For a moment his hand continued to rest, with liquid heat, on her shoulder. Just long enough for her to feel a strange melting sensation of panic. She couldn't *make* him not touch her. She saw her unsettling primal awareness of his greater strength register in his eyes, and, his point made, his hand fell away.

"Let's get a few things straight," he said, his voice smooth and unruffled, those incredibly clear, cold gray eyes fastening on her face and holding her unwilling captive. "I've got a job to do, and I'm going to do it. It'll be far easier for both of us if you cooperate."

She felt she had lost ground, and she scrambled to make it up. "I'm sure you'll manage just fine without my cooperation, and, since you want to go over the ground rules, you might keep in mind that I'm not accustomed to being addressed flippantly."

"Pardon me," he said, unperturbed, "for thinking that a touch of humor might reduce the tension in an unpleasant situation. I won't make the effort again, Miss Paige."

"Well, if your comment about the Congressman was your idea of humor, I certainly hope you won't!"

"I won't," he promised, "and I won't be addressed like a wayward puppy again, either." His voice was soft and warm and sensuous as velvet, even as his eyes came one degree closer to freezing. "Don't ever use that tone of voice to me again."

"Don't you presume to tell me what tone of voice to use!" she snapped. "My life has been quite messed up enough without having to guard against your sensitivities!"

"So," he surmised with quiet steel in his voice, "I'm not to address you with anything but formal correctness, and you can address me any way you want."

She could see in his eyes that he thought she was one of those rich, spoiled women who stamped all over people with relish. Nothing could be further from the truth, but she had no intention of correcting him.

She shrugged. "You're the one with the job to do."

He nodded. "And I'll do it. And you, Miss Paige, will not make it unpleasant for me." He said that with insufferable self-assurance.

Devon cocked an eyebrow at him. "And, pray tell, what would you do if I did?" she mocked.

He took one more step toward her, and his physical nearness brought the blood hammering to her throat. She found herself retreating from some unspoken and very masculine threat for the second time in as many minutes. She wasn't sure exactly what the danger was, but she knew it existed.

"If you ever lay a hand on me *again*, I'll have you fired!" she hissed, hoping the absolute authority of her tone would hide her hammering heart.

"I don't have the kind of job that it's easy to get fired from, Miss Paige." He eyed her thoughtfully. "As for laying a hand on you, the days when a good spanking would have done you some good are probably long past. All the same, your life could well depend on my knowing exactly when to put my hands on you."

She had barely recovered from the odd intimacy of that statement when he continued, his voice soft as suede.

"Don't lock horns with me, Miss Paige. You won't win, and I don't have the patience for it." His eyes caught on her lips with succinct threat. "And I don't deal with a difficult woman by brutalizing her," he drawled.

She couldn't prevent the horrified widening of her eyes. He cocked his head at her in barely noticeable assent. She stared at him in disbelief, wanting to look anywhere except his lips. And yet it was his lips her appalled gaze attached to—hard lips. Firm. Relentless. An electric shiver wrenched the soft flesh in the region of her belly, shocking her. She forced her nearly paralyzed eyes to meet his. His were glittering wickedly, and she had the awful feeling he found her momentarily amusing, as if he had seen through the thin veneer of her aggressive sophistication to an innocence he wouldn't hesitate to use against her.

"I detest men who have an inflated view of the power their self-proclaimed prowess gives them over women." Her voice came out surprisingly brave and convincing.

He looked faintly amused. "I'm not sure I even know what you just said."

"If you ever try to kiss me, I'll...I'll bite your nose!"

"Kiss you?" He raised his eyebrows with a cold mockery that made her feel utterly foolish. "I don't recall saying anything about kissing you. I don't recall even using the word 'kiss.'"

Devon felt heat creep up her cheeks. "You just said you didn't deal with difficult women by brutalizing them!"

"I don't. But it's quite an interesting leap in logic to assume I meant I'd kiss them."

She glared at him helplessly. What could she do? Shriek accusingly that he'd been staring at her lips?

She tossed her head carelessly. "So how do you deal with difficult women?"

He shrugged, with an aggravating lack of interest. "I guess if you choose to be difficult, you'll find out. But you won't be difficult, will you?"

She planted her hands solidly on her hips. "Don't bet on it!"

"Look," he said quietly, his forceful eyes still holding hers captive, "I'm just doing my job. I don't have any more choice about this than you do."

She did not like being told she didn't have choices. Come to think of it, she did not like one single thing about the man who stood so solidly in front of her, his arms folded across the barrel of his solid chest.

But in a flash she saw that it was not to her advantage to let him see that. If she was going to "win," and she fully intended to, then she needed him to be relaxed. She needed that wary alertness to disappear from his eyes. She had taken exactly the wrong tack by letting him see her hostility, and now she backtracked.

"I suppose there's no sense fighting it," she said. She debated a docile sigh and decided never to make the mistake of playing this man for a fool.

Even without the sigh, her statement, rather than lessening the suspicion in those clear eyes, intensified it. The faintest of frowns touched the firm lines of his mouth and creased his forehead. His very frown goaded her, made the good girl in her want to be very, very bad. She did not want a bodyguard. She had worked too hard and too long to achieve a life-style that was starting to approximate to normal.

"I didn't catch your name," she said, deliberately keeping some stiffness in her tone. He was altogether too alert. Several hundred hours of drama training wouldn't fool him for a second. He had the kind of eyes that probed deeper than words, and even deeper than actions, piercing eyes that seemed to search her own eyes for all the secrets of her soul.

Except for those searing eyes, his expression was a study in blandness. "Carmichael."

"Is that your first name?" She allowed some of the stiffness to leave her voice, and began to shift subtly into a role she played rather well—the charming, faintly flirtatious young socialite that her father wanted so badly for her to be.

"No, it isn't."

"Do you have a first name?"

"Yes, I do." But he didn't volunteer it.

Devon felt the slight of him not offering his name to the bottom of her toes. Grimly she reminded herself not to let any hostility toward him show. She reminded herself that he couldn't possibly snub her unless she showed him who she really was, which she had no intention of doing. Very few people who had any relationship with her father were allowed to see Devon as she was—quiet, sensitive, thoughtful, caring.

"And do you ever smile?" she asked sweetly, continuing the game.

"Yes, I do." But he didn't.

"This isn't going to be a lot of fun, is it?" she pouted.

"No," he said flatly.

His insinuation that he was going to have even less fun than her made her feel hurt despite her vow not to allow him to hurt her, and made her hide behind her role even more.

"Well, if we're going to be stuck together couldn't you at least try to be agreeable?" she chided.

"I don't get paid to be agreeable. Sorry. Just your typical goon, I guess."

"You heard that." She saw his baiting her in a slightly more understandable light, though she didn't forgive him for it.

He gave her a disbelieving look.

"I'm sorry if I hurt your feelings." She *was* faintly sorry if she'd hurt his feelings, though she severely doubted if he possessed such a commodity. She was more interested in winning a modicum of trust from him . . . a trust she would abuse by slipping out of his grasp the moment he relaxed.

"You didn't hurt my feelings," he told her. "I'd have to care about you before you could hurt my feelings."

She'd known the minute she saw this man that she didn't like him. Disliking had deepened to detesting in a matter of minutes, and now she was fairly certain for the first time in her life that she hated someone. So why did it sting when he returned the very same sentiment?

"Well," she said stiffly, "if you don't care about me, what difference does it make to you if somebody kidnaps me or shoots me or blows up the house, or whatever the supposed threat was?"

He shrugged, that wicked glitter in his eyes again, branding her a difficult little girl whom he obviously considered himself more than a match for.

"It might reflect on how well I'd done my job, if I let any of those things happen," he commented dryly. "I'm very good at my job."

He'd just made her feel like "the goods." She might as well have been a sack of potatoes he'd been given to guard!

His eyes had let go of hers now, and they were straying up and down the hall, narrow and cautious. His voice was coldly polite when he spoke again. "If I could, I'll get you to show me the house and the grounds. I need to ask you some questions about your friends and acquaintances. After that, I'll do my best to fade into the woodwork. Most of the time, you won't even know I'm around."

Devon took in the immense breadth of those shoulders, the rugged cut of his face, the disturbing glitter in his eyes. Nobody was ever going to forget this man was around!

She had no intention, of course, of making life easy for him by giving in to his every demand. The trick was going to be to make it seem as if she would concur if she could, and that it was just circumstances that prevented her from being the model of cooperation.

"Actually, could the tour wait?" She struggled to match his coolly polite tone. "Or maybe one of the servants could do it. I have a splitting headache, and I'd like to lie down for a while."

His face was an impregnable fortress of solid rock. He nodded, with supreme uncaring, though she suddenly noticed the faint flickering of a small muscle in his jaw. She hid a satisfied smile. *Are you winning so far, Mr. Carmichael?*

He stayed her hand on the doorknob of her room. "I'll go in first," he said quietly.

"Oh, really!" she snapped, snatching her hand back as though he'd accidentally touched her with a branding iron.

He went into the room, and she followed him, her arms folded over her chest. "Any bogeys?" she queried.

He gave her a cutting look, then his gaze flicked around the room. Devon felt oddly stripped, as if the nubby pink and obviously aged teddy bear on her bedspread and the collection of wildly romantic books on her bedside table told him things about her that she did not want him to know.

His slow, searching gaze had already moved on, and he went to the window, studied the latch, locked it, and moved to the French doors that opened on to her balcony.

He turned back to her. "Keep the window and the door locked," he said crisply.

"And what if I want fresh air?" she demanded, reacting almost instinctively to his high-handedness. Fight or flight. The man had a knack for making her behave like a cornered shrew. She didn't seem to have any happy medium in her repertoire, even though she was probably sabotaging her own escape by getting his back up.

That fascinating muscle in his jaw jerked again, though his voice was smooth with professional indifference. "If you want fresh air, just tell me and I'll see that someone is posted underneath your window."

She absolutely did not want somebody posted outside her window! "Oh, no," she said hastily. "I just wondered."

He gave her a piercing look, and she attempted to smile brightly.

He turned his big back on her and went out the door. Just as she was allowing the strange tension he caused in her begin to uncoil, he turned back to her.

"If," he informed her, his voice dispassionate, "in some moment of incomprehensible madness, I ever decided to kiss you, the last thing on your mind would be biting my nose."

He stepped out through the door and shut it softly behind him.

Devon stood for a moment in stunned silence. The sudden absence of his presence made her acutely aware of what a powerful force he was to contend with.

She knew instantly what she had to do, and felt quite giddy with the audacity of what she was planning. On silent feet she crossed her bedroom to the French door he had locked, and lifted the latch. She stepped out, scanned the grounds and then with devilish delight hoisted herself over the railing, tucked her skirt in between her legs, wrapped her long, slender limbs around a supporting pillar and slid to the ground as she had done a hundred times before.

If, she rationalized, you ever let a man like that get the upper hand, *trouble* would have to be redefined.

CHAPTER TWO

DEVON reentered the house by the front door and slammed it—hard. Mischief was only fun if it was noticed.

As far as she could tell, her disappearance, rather than causing an amusing uproar, had gone completely unobserved. She stood expectantly in the entrance foyer. Any second, someone, and with luck Carmichael himself, would come thundering in here and ask where the devil she had been, so she could announce with casual glee that she had been out for her stroll.

The seconds ticked by, and it was evident nobody was "thundering" in this house. Devon felt a ridiculous surge of anger.

"The incompetent fools," she muttered. "The front door wasn't even locked!"

Signs of incompetence should, she reminded herself, be making her feel nearly delirious with relief, since it was evident she was going to have no problem slipping the leash when the time came.

She momentarily considered getting her weekend bag and car keys right now and disappearing a few days earlier than planned. That should deflate the balloon-size ego of Mr. Carmichael.

She smiled. But why do things in a small way? She could really put him in his place if she waited a few days, and lulled him into a sense of complacency before she bade him adieu. There was no sense changing her plans to accommodate this little crisis in her life. That would be like letting them win. And she had just seen that it was going to be easy to leave any time she wanted.

She heard the patio door, that opened off the library, slide open and then the low murmur of male voices. Probably a truckload full of terrorists piling in the side doors, she told herself wryly, moving in that direction.

She went into the library—and stopped short. Two men she didn't know were sitting on opposite sides of the desk talking in low tones. On a dark leather sofa that sat in the center of the room facing the fireplace was her *protector*—fast asleep. Her annoyance, irrationally, deepened.

The two other men were scrambling to their feet.

"Good guys, I presume?" said Devon, folding her arms across her chest and forcing her eyes not to stray to that figure on the sofa. She had seen quite enough. For instance, he looked younger asleep, relaxed. The hardness, the wariness were erased from his face. A lock of that neat hair had fallen over his forehead.

"Phil Moriarty, ma'am."

"Michael Wilson."

She enjoyed the way they were looking at her, especially the younger one, Michael Wilson. She usually had this effect on men because she was such a typical California girl—tall, tanned, blond and willowy. She supposed she was enjoying it even more because it was exactly the sort of reaction she hadn't got from *him.*

Despite her best effort her eyes did stray back to the couch. Sleeping, those intriguing hints of darkness, of danger, were gone from him. Now he looked deceptively clean-cut. Captain of the football team. Apple pie and ice cream. All American——

"Grey!" Wilson reached over the back of the sofa and gave Carmichael's shoulder a shake.

Devon was just registering the name Grey, rolling it over in her mind, realizing how much it suited her enigmatic protector, when she saw Michael Wilson fly over the sofa and land hard on his back on the floor in front of it.

Grey Carmichael was off the sofa, and had one knee planted at Wilson's throat.

Devon registered the stunned fear in Wilson's face, and gasped from the shock of how quickly the all-American image was shattered. Grey Carmichael was a commando, tough and brutal, and for a split second everyone in the room was absolutely aware of it. Not so much as a breath disturbed the frozen stillness.

Grey Carmichael looked down into the younger man's face, and blinked. And then the panther-coiled tightness left his body, and he leapt lithely to his feet. He held out a hand, and pulled Michael Wilson to his feet.

"Jeez, kid," he said gruffly. "Sorry." He shook his head. "I'm just back from a tough haul in Central America, and I haven't acclimatized. I was supposed to get some leave, but..." He shrugged and shook his head again. "You okay?"

Michael Wilson nodded, a trifle shakily. "I'm fine." His voice was a squeak.

Grey Carmichael's eyes, fully alert now, fell on Devon. "Good afternoon, ma'am," he said, apparently unconcerned and unembarrassed that she had just witnessed that scene. "Have a nice *rest*?"

She frowned slightly at his emphasis, then thought she had probably imagined it. She was feeling somewhat rattled by the incident she had just witnessed, as well as from the fact that he seemed to make the leap from being a man with killer-honed instincts to being a man of smooth politeness with a remarkable lack of effort.

"Not as nice as yours, I warrant," she said tightly.

"Umm." He turned to Phil Moriarty, asking something with his eyes. The other man nodded, ever so slightly, and Grey Carmichael turned back to her.

"This is Phil Moriarty. You'll be seeing him around—he's part of the security team. And this is——"

"We've met," Devon said coolly. "Fortunately, Mr. Moriarty and Mr. Wilson both look like good guys, and not terrorists, so I didn't try to defend myself by cracking vases over their heads . . . while you were napping."

"It was your need for a nap, not mine, that prevented you from being introduced to the team. And from now on, ask to see ID if you see someone you don't know on the premises. Good guys and bad guys look remarkably alike."

"Oh? And what do bad guys do when asked for their ID? Wait for the bodyguard to wake up so they can present their credentials properly?"

Grey Carmichael sighed. "I'm suggesting you use a modicum of caution, if you think you can manage that. And Phil had everything under control while I caught a few 'z's.'"

Devon was tempted to tell him she could have tunneled to China and back while Phil was in charge, but she didn't want to get Phil into trouble—nor do anything to make the security team become overly zealous in the performance of their duties.

Her eyes widened on Grey Carmichael. He had reached casually underneath his jacket. He shrugged his shoulders and she caught a glimpse of the harness he was adjusting.

He was wearing a gun! No wonder Mike Wilson was still looking green around the gills. He hadn't thought he was about to be handed a handkerchief!

His hand dropped abruptly from under the jacket and his eyes met hers levelly. "This isn't a game designed to inconvenience you. You might want to remember that."

She realized that not once had it occurred to her to take this supposed threat seriously. The brief glimpse of that very real gun had introduced the hideous possibility that her world was no longer safe. Not that she intended to give him the satisfaction of knowing a shadow of doubt had entered her world. Not that she intended to do one single thing differently than she ever had. Her father had been trying for years, unsuccessfully, to make her a prisoner of fear.

"Now, why don't you give me that tour of the house?" Grey continued.

She grudgingly agreed, and he seemed to find her acquiescence amusing. Either that, or his sleep had put him in better humor. Because he smiled at her. His smile was dazzling—simply dazzling. Straight teeth flashed brilliantly white against the bronze of his skin, and a deep crease, that might have been called a dimple on another man, sliced up the side of his face.

"What would you like to see first, Mr. Carmichael?" Devon sniffed.

"Let's just make it Grey," he suggested. He locked his hands behind his head for a minute and thrust his chest forward in the most sensuous stretch she had ever witnessed.

"Grey," she agreed in a clipped tone, watching him with narrow-eyed suspicion. He was turning on all that powerful male charisma quite deliberately. Turning on the charm to try and turn the difficult woman into putty in his hands, no doubt. Egomaniac!

Well, she could play his game, for as long as it suited her. But oh, what satisfaction it was going to give her to put a gash in his rather infuriating sense of confidence! He acted as if he was a man accustomed to having the whole world bow down and beg to do his bidding. He was a man who needed to be taught a lesson.

"Why don't we go bottom to top?" he suggested. "Basement to attic?"

"I'm not going into the basement," she told him delicately. "There are cobwebs down there." These self-same cobwebs, of course, had lent "mood" to her fabulously imaginative childhood games, and she wasn't the least afraid of them.

"And forget the attic too," she continued. "Bats." She had never seen a bat in her life, and certainly not in the attic, which had also been a favorite childhood haunt.

"Any other areas you're sensitive to?" he asked dryly. "You might want to be careful the flour dust in the kitchen doesn't ruin your silk blouse. And you have to be careful of African violet allergies. I think I saw some of those purple death mongers in the living room."

Devon wondered, briefly, how a man who looked as rugged as the Rocky Mountains knew the difference between cotton and silk. She supposed it was nothing more than a lucky guess, just as he was guessing that she wasn't really afraid of cobwebs or bats.

He went down into the basement by himself. She conducted an indifferent tour of the rest of the house for him.

"Is this milk chute used?" he asked.

Devon shrugged helplessly. "I didn't even know there was a milk chute there."

"Is this porch lit at night...? Do you come in this room often...? When...? What do you do here...? What lights are on?" And all the time he was firing questions at her, his eyes were moving, assessing, judging. From time to time his notebook would come out and he'd jot down the location of a broken window lock. If she hadn't evaded him with such ease earlier, she might have actually felt confidence in his ability to protect her.

He tried every door, and every window, opening and shutting them with his head cocked as if he were memorizing the sound. He inspected the alarm systems, and the latches.

Devon began to find his thoroughness irritating. "For goodness' sake, are you memorizing the contents of every room?" she demanded.

He didn't look at her, and he answered absently. "That's exactly what I'm doing—memorizing. Entrances, exits, windows, locks, hiding places, light switches, obstacles—hazards."

"One expects a secret agent's life to be rather more exciting," she told him.

"I'm not a secret agent." He said this as if she was a bothersome gnat that he could hardly waste the effort to shoo away. "And *I'm* not bored."

"Well, that makes one of us."

"Pardon me for taking half an hour of your valuable time in the event it might help me protect your life and limb." His voice was only mildly sarcastic. "What am I keeping you from? Something wildly important like a tanning session by the pool?"

He swung around and looked at her quizzically, as though it interested him to have such a superficial specimen of the life form in the same room as him available for study.

For a moment Devon struggled. It would be so easy to spit out the truth, to tell him that she had ruined her father's dreams for her by becoming a schoolteacher. And that she spent her days, not sunning herself by a pool, but in a steaming hot classroom in the dead center of Los Angeles's teeming inner city.

Unfortunately, the moment's satisfaction she would gain by the surprise, and perhaps even respect, that would show on his face would be far outweighed by the fact that her escape route would be cut off. And who knew what new schemes her father might be capable of when Grey Carmichael shared with him information he would find so totally threatening? She could just picture herself arriving at her school one morning to see it ringed with Daddy's private army... or worse. Misused influence could be far reaching.

She bit her lip, and scowled at Grey.

"Here," he offered, catching her by surprise, because his deep voice held an unexpected note of patience, "I'll show you what I'm doing and why it's important."

He reached over and switched off the light. Devon hadn't realized how completely night had fallen, and the darkness startled her.

"Turn the light on," she ordered. "I'm not that interested."

"Are you afraid of the dark?" He had moved, his voice nearer to her than he had been a moment ago.

She was not afraid of the dark. She just found the dark unfamiliar and disturbing with him sharing it with her.

"Let's just say you and I are sitting here having tea one night——" he went on.

"That's a highly unlikely scenario," she interrupted, moving toward the wall and groping for the light switch.

"—when the lights go out. Stop looking for the switch and listen to me. It's not on that wall, anyway."

"I told you, I'm not that interested." How was it he could see her fumbling around for the light switch, and she had only the faintest notion where he was?

"I suggest you manage a little curiosity. This will take three minutes. And the information I give you could save your life."

"How desperately melodramatic!" She folded her arms across her chest, giving up the hunt for the light switch. She thought he was right—it was on the other wall. And where was he now?

There was a long pause. "Are you listening?" he asked again, his voice no-nonsense.

"Yes," she snapped.

"If the lights go out, you hit the deck. If I'm close, I'll remind you. I'd say something like, 'Devon, get down.' Flat on the floor, as quickly as you can. Do you understand that?''

"It would depend on what I was wearing," she responded flippantly, her flippancy partially in reaction to the fact that his voice in the darkness had a disturbing quality, like a too hot summer evening. But her name came off his lips like a breath of fresh air off the ocean, smooth and calm.

She gasped when he touched her. She hadn't heard him cross the room to her. His hand was resting on the back of her neck. She could feel the strength in it, the leashed power in the light touch of his fingers on the hairs at the nape of her neck.

"Now, I know you don't listen very well," he chided her, something in his voice still evoking thoughts of restless hot nights and trickling sweat, "so I know I'm probably going to have to help you get down."

"What makes you think I don't listen?" she argued. He was so close to her she could smell him—a good smell, clean and hot, like soap and sunshine mingling together. An intimate smell that again put her mind to the sultriness of summer evenings.

"The second thing I'm going to tell you is to shut up, and I won't be polite about it."

"Surprise, surprise," she retorted sarcastically. Her heart was beating erratically now. It was too close in here. She had no intention of ever letting him guess she found this experience entirely too unsettling. "Besides, the lights have gone out and I'm lying on the floor. It's probably not the moment I'd choose to start whistling *Dixie* or——"

A hand covered her mouth. His hand was hard against the softness of her lips. His skin had a taste, like raindrops, and a texture, like steel sheathed in silk. His other hand went flat against her back. He pushed her, with gentle but insistent strength, down onto her knees and then onto her front.

He took his hand away from her mouth.

"I should have bitten you!" she hissed. Uneasy adrenaline pumped through her veins because of his nearness, because of this oddly exciting game they were playing, because the drugging taste of his skin still tingled on her lips.

"Hmm, you could have. But I don't want to discuss your fetish about biting right now——"

"My fetish!" she squeaked. "My——"

His hand covered her mouth again. His tone changed, and she could hear the sternness in it. "This is business, Devon, and it's important. I want your undivided attention."

He slid his hand away from her mouth. She could make out the ghostly outline of his face. It was devoid of humor, absolutely and chillingly formidable in the velvety darkness. He was once again the commando who had come awake with survival on his mind. He knew about survival. Her voice had dried up in her throat. She couldn't have spoken if she wanted to.

Grey tapped the coffee table in front of her nose. "Natural obstacle. I wouldn't want to smack you into something like this when I pull you down. But I might want to use it for cover."

He was sitting on his haunches, the moonlight glancing off his strong, serious features. "Now, if you had to get out of here fast, which way would go you?"

She pointed to the nearest door.

"That's the obvious way—obvious to everybody, unfortunately. I want you to try thinking in terms of light and shadow. Do you want to be going by that window, even crouched?''

"No, I suppose not," she said. It occurred to her that this was truly scary. That in actual fact he was teaching her how to outwit an assailant, how to survive. It should have been unnerving, but she felt strangely exhilarated. Was that why he did a job like this? For that pump of adrenaline that was flowing through her veins, making all her senses sizzle with something very oddly like sensuality?

She looked at the room again. "I'd go that way," she said, pointing at the pool of shadow between two sofas. "And into the bathroom. And out of the window."

His teeth flashed white against the darkness. "Good girl! That's exactly the exit route I came up with for this room."

Devon felt enormously pleased with herself. "Don't call me a girl, unless you want to be called a boy!" she retorted.

Grey ignored this. "Do you know what a tiger crawl is?"

"Oh, sure. We practiced it daily at finishing school."

"I'll demonstrate," he said, not seeming too amused by her comment. He dropped down onto his stomach, and used his elbows to propel himself between the two sofas. "Now you do it."

"Are you kidding?"

"No."

"I'm wearing a skirt, for heaven's sake!" she protested.

"That is not an acceptable excuse."

"I am not a flunky in your private army, Mr. Carmichael, and I am not crawling around on the floor with my skirt riding up around my hips for your general amusement," Devon told him firmly.

"Oh." She could hear masculine comprehension dawning in his voice. She allowed herself a moment's relief, not to mention a small, smug smile. Her skirt probably wouldn't ride *that* high. Her victory was rather short-lived.

"Okay, I won't look," he promised.

"If you aren't looking how will you know if I'm doing it properly?" she parried.

"Has anybody ever told you you're damned near impossible?" he hissed.

"Never quite so nicely," she responded sweetly.

"Devon——" his face appeared out of the darkness not four inches from her face, and she nearly shrieked, despite the fact that his tone was once again reflecting only complete and cool professionalism "—you're lucky enough to have a chance for a dress rehearsal. If anything goes wrong, and you've done this drill once, there's a small chance things would come back to you in a crisis. You've got a teaching degree. How do people learn? By listening to other people talk? Or by trying things themselves?"

Anger she could handle with aplomb. Rationality was a little more difficult. She'd been out-talked and she knew it. Muttering epithets she certainly had not learned in finishing school, she crawled across the floor. It was certainly harder than he had made it look, but she managed to wriggle over the same course as him with her dignity—and her skirt—intact. Then Grey jumped lithely back to his feet, went over and turned on the light. He came back and helped her to stand up. She could see the commando in him again, no-nonsense, emotionless.

"Sometimes I use hand signals. This is down." He brought his right arm down sharply from his shoulder, his hand flat to the ground. "And this is quiet." He slashed his hand across his throat. "If we have a threat, you have to remember a few things. I'm the boss—that's the most important one. No questions, no back talk. And down. And quiet. You got that?"

Devon folded her arms across her chest. "How did you know I had a teaching degree?" she asked.

He sighed, a deep sound of long suffering. "First things first. What's important?"

"How you knew about my degree." The look on his face was deadly and dangerous. "Okay, okay! Down. And quiet."

"Who's the boss, Devon?" His voice was quiet, its very quietness making it ultimately intimidating.

"Oh, all right," she snapped. "In the unlikely event of a terrorist attack, or trouble with the hydro wires masquerading as a terrorist attack, Mr. Grey Carmichael is the boss. Does that make you happy? Would you like me to open the window and shout it out for the neighbors to hear? Would that assuage your large masculine ego?"

"Get something straight, Devon Paige," he gritted, "this little exercise has nothing to do with my ego, and everything to do with your safety."

She tossed her head. "Oh, pooh! What are the chances of this being a real threat as opposed to a letter from some crank?" *Or even a plot by my father.* "One in a million?"

"I always assume that threats of this nature are serious—dead serious. To do anything else is to invite trouble and tragedy."

"Humph. Have you seen the letters?" she asked him.

"No."

"Why not?" she demanded.

"I only get information myself on a 'need to know' basis. You don't need to know," Grey explained.

"I think it would be appropriate for me to evaluate the threat myself," she said peevishly.

"People more qualified than you have already evaluated the threat. It exists—that's all you need to know. Sorry." He didn't sound very sorry.

"How did you know about my teaching degree?" *And what else do you know?* Surely he couldn't have information that she didn't even allow her father to have?

"I'm telepathic," he said blandly. "Plus I have a little file with your name on it. You were born in Mount of Angels Hospital, and spent the first five years of your life in a modest little bungalow on Glendale Road. Your mother died when you were three. Your father began to realize some of his ambition just as you were entering school, so you were educated at private schools. There was a series of house changes, each reflecting your father's changing status, with Redwoods being the last. You went on to a women's university. You graduated with an Honors degree in Education. You speak French—badly—your best friend's name is Bonnie Johnson, and," he paused wickedly, "you've never had a boyfriend."

"I do not speak French *badly*!" she informed him coolly, utterly dismayed by how much he knew about her. She switched to French. "And I have had a boyfriend."

"Possibly," he agreed. He switched to French too. "The last two years of your life are somewhat of a blank, a fact I hope to rectify over the next few days."

He didn't comment on her French—he didn't have to. It was deplorable in comparison to his.

"Anyway," he taunted her softly, "I can't wait to hear all about your 'boyfriend.' In the next few days, we'll start going over the people in your life with a fine-tooth comb."

Devon smiled at him. Of course, the possibility of that was daunting, but she didn't plan to be here in the next few days.

"I hope you're not easily shocked," she said silkily.

"I'm not," he said dryly.

Not, of course, that she really did have anything shocking to disclose, but it was rather fun to hint that she did when she was never going to have to reveal the truth. The truth was she had had boyfriends, and all kinds of them too. The other fact was that they were just what that name would suggest—males who were friends, nothing more.

Her father had invited the men to have dinner with them, and Michael Wilson and Grey had accepted. The younger man, Mike Wilson, was looking at her with the puppy-dog look she was more accustomed to, and she set about charming him. But with every low laugh and flutter of her eyelashes she was saying to Grey Carmichael, I've had four million boy friends, not that you're ever going to know the difference.

Dinner drew to a merciful close. Mike Wilson looked as if he would lie down on the floor and let her walk on him, a fact that Grey Carmichael seemed to be taking in with displeasure.

"Miss Paige, I'll need your schedule for tomorrow," was all he said, though, as he rose, he seemed to give Mike Wilson a warning look.

"I'm going to go shopping," she said.

He nodded with curt indifference.

"Devon, are you going to ride with me in the morning?" he father asked.

For a moment she was going to say no, except that she noticed that Grey Carmichael had frozen behind his chair, his knuckles white against the back of the chair.

The man had a deathly fear of horses, unless she missed her guess! Imagine a man like that having weaknesses, just as she did. Imagine him practically forcing her to do his stupid crawl in between couches. Well, turnabout was fair play.

"I think I will ride with you in the morning," she said with wicked delight. "I guess you'll be joining us, will you, Grey?" she asked sweetly.

"Not if I can help it," he answered, and turned and walked away from the table.

"You know how to ride, don't you, Wilson?"

"Me? Are you kidding, Grey? I grew up in Chicago."

"Great!" Grey sighed fatalistically. "Go track down Moriarty and see if he can ride."

Wilson came back a few minutes later. "Says he wouldn't know one end from the other."

"Hell!"

"Do you want me to go tell Miss Paige they'll have to cancel their ride?" Wilson asked eagerly.

"Quit looking for excuses to be around Dev—Miss Paige," Grey told him brusquely. "You don't mix romance with this kind of business."

"I wasn't," Wilson denied sulkily.

"Fine. See that you don't."

"What about their ride?"

"I'll go," Grey snapped tersely.

"But not like it much?" the younger man guessed.

"I hate horses."

"Really?"

"I spent two weeks in a Russian prison once—and I'd rather do that again than have to ride a horse."

"But you know how to ride?"

"Yeah. I just don't like it."

"I'm sure if you explained that to Mr. Paige——"

"Look, Wilson, there's a psychology involved in protecting people. As little disruption to their routines as possible. Letting them keep as much normality as they can. Coming in and going out so you do as little lasting damage as possible. We're trained for this kind of stuff, paid for it. They're not. He thinks this whole thing is a game, and she doesn't believe it. And that's fine. It keeps them calm and functioning. This job will get a little harder if the panic hits.

"Besides, I'm in enough hot water with the Colonel without word filtering back to him that I didn't go riding because I didn't *feel* like it."

"You're in hot water with the Colonel? Maybe I should have guessed that. This isn't the kind of job you usually land, is it?"

"Not usually," Grey agreed.

"But it's not a bad job," Wilson said, "is it?"

"No," said Grey. "Sofa's soft, and the coffee's hot. What more could a man want?" *To make the world a better place.* He didn't say it. No use the word getting around that he was still an idealist after all these years. That he lived for those rare moments of down-to-the-bone satisfaction that this job gave him in a way no other job on earth ever could. A feeling that he suspected he wasn't going to get from this particular assignment. The girl had probably been right—not that he'd ever tell her, or ever let his guard down. The chances of a real threat were pretty slim.

"I don't think you should have to ride horses if you don't like them," Wilson said with that youthful lack of awareness of how the world *really* ran.

"You're so green, Wilson," Grey sighed wearily. "You like jumping out of airplanes?"

"Not much," Wilson admitted.

"You do it anyway?"

"I had to, on my training."

"That's what this job is about, Wilson. Functioning even though you're scared spitless." Grey sighed. "But you don't have to like it." His big shoulders heaved. "And, God, I just hate horses!"

CHAPTER THREE

DEVON met her father going back to the house just as she was heading for the stables. She noted that he was carrying his cordless phone and knew before he said anything that some sort of corporate crisis had developed.

He feigned deep regret over missing the ride, but she knew he thrived on emergencies.

She debated, briefly, whether to cancel the ride. She didn't want to spend an hour in Grey's company. On the other hand, she'd probably be in his company whether they rode or not, and opportunities to pay him back for his high-handedness yesterday were not going to be popping up on trees.

Besides, she was wearing a simply sumptuous, curve-hugging riding outfit, that would no doubt make him want to check himself into the psychiatric ward for even suggesting she might never have had a boy friend.

She rounded the corner of the stable and slammed right into him.

"Watch where you're going!" she remonstrated sharply.

"Good morning, little Miss Sunshine," he said, removing his steadying hands from her shoulders.

"Don't apologize," she snapped, "I wasn't hurt."

"I won't apologize," Grey came back calmly, "because *I* wasn't barreling around as if the barn were on fire."

Never, Devon thought blackly, had the allure of curve-molding breeches been more wasted.

He had already dismissed her, and was looking back at the map in his hands.

She squandered a regal glare on him before she wandered over to where the horses were saddled, and while pretending to adjust a girth, she studied him. This morning he was dressed in faded jeans, which molded the clean long length of his legs. A knit sports shirt stretched across the breadth of his chest, hugging the granite cut of his pectoral muscles. The shirt-sleeves were short, ending midway over a sinewy mound of biceps. His arms were brown, whipcord hard. She turned her gaze determinedly back to the horse, though her thoughts were not so easily directed.

Grey Carmichael was in disgustingly good shape for a man who looked to be in his mid-thirties. Add to that the rugged cut of his features, and the smoky intensity of those eyes, and she supposed you had a fairly attractive kind of man. Which was no doubt exactly why he had such an inflated idea of himself. Well, he wasn't her type, and she'd do her utmost to bring him down a peg or two before she had to leave him.

"I'll consider it my sacred duty to the sisterhood of women," she muttered to herself.

"What?"

She nearly jumped out of her skin. She spun around. "Must you sneak about like that?" she snapped. "Is that part of your job training—sneaking? Do you spend long hours creeping through forests without making a sound until you perfect the art of——"

"If you didn't chatter away like a monkey, even when you don't have a soul to inflict yourself on, you would have heard me," Grey commented dryly.

"You're entirely too impudent, Mr. Carmichael," she told him coldly. "I have a mind to report you to your superiors."

"My superiors," he said, with an unconcerned grin, "are well aware of my shortcomings, particularly in the area of impudence—which is probably why I'm standing here with several of the most detestable creatures God ever created, instead of taking part in an operation I spent two years of my life helping to set up."

"Detestable?" she echoed, her voice much smaller than she would have liked.

"I was referring to the horses," he told her with just a trace of kindness.

As if she needed his kindness! "Well, I certainly didn't think you were referring to me," she said with a toss of her head. "Not that I would have cared if you were."

"Hmm."

"Could we go, please?" she suggested icily.

He shrugged. "Sure. I rode some of the trails with the groom this morning, looking for possible trouble spots. How does this look for a route?"

Devon took the map he passed her, very aware that she avoided even the most casual contact with his hand. A red pencil mark showed where he had ridden. He'd done at least two hours of riding already! She wondered if she'd been mistaken about his fear of horses, but he'd just confirmed that he detested them. She studied his face; she noticed it was unusually pale. She also noticed a tenseness in the way he held himself that was completely at odds with how fluid and at ease he had seemed yesterday.

"That looks fine," she said.

He carefully folded the map and slipped it into the back pocket of his jeans. She had the funny idea that his preoccupation with the map might have been stalling for time.

"Can I help you up?" he offered.

"No, thanks." Devon vaulted into the saddle. She was an excellent horsewoman—horses being about the only part of her father's affluence that she enjoyed.

She watched Grey from the saddle, and noticed he turned away from her to mount himself, and that he fiddled with the girth for a long time. She saw his shoulders give a great heave, before he lowered the stirrup and pulled himself with easy strength into the saddle.

His jaw was definitely clenched very hard, she thought, but he met her questioning gaze without any expression at all. They set out, and out of the corner of her eye she noted that Grey rode well, but with a certain unmistakable rigidity. Somehow his misery was not making her nearly as gleeful as she had imagined it would.

"So tell me about your job," she suggested. "If this isn't usual for you, what is?" she asked. She realized she was trying to get his mind off his distress, partly because she felt a small twinge of guilt in the part she had played in causing it.

"Oh, a day at the office might include dodging a few bullets, running down some Mafioso, rescuing a maiden in distress, getting a kitten down from a tree, drinking a few fingers of whisky and rolling into bed with an unbelievably beautiful woman who's really a Russian spy."

"Thank you for taking me so seriously!"

"You just have no sense of humor."

"Pardon me for not thinking it's uproariously funny to be mocked."

"I wasn't mocking *you*," he explained. "If anything, I might have been mocking myself. My job is basically tough, lonely and boring. Occasionally a lot of very tedious legwork will have a big payoff that makes me fall in love with what I do all over again."

"But this time you're missing the payoff," she guessed. "What's the big operation you mentioned?"

"That's the other thing about my job—I can't talk about it a lot. The operation is a secret. In a few days it'll probably be in the papers where we can both read all about it."

"Drugs," she guessed.

Grey cut her a surprised look. "What makes you say that?"

"Yesterday, you said you'd been in Central America. What else could it be?"

"Illegal imports of alligator-skin purses?" he suggested.

She ignored him. "So how come you aren't going to be allowed in on the bust?"

He smiled at her easy use of a term popularized by television. "Ah, you might say I was talking when I should have been listening."

"That's all? Goodness, I'm glad I don't have a job like that!"

"You wouldn't last a day," he agreed wryly.

They rode on in silence for a few minutes.

"You ride quite well," Devon finally commented carefully.

"Do I?" he said noncommittally.

"Do you ride often?"

"I haven't been on a horse in twenty years."

And he hoped he wouldn't be on one for another twenty, she guessed, feeling a growing sympathy for him.

"You're going to have a sore behind tomorrow," she said, then felt her cheeks heat. She really didn't want to even think about his behind, or the way it had looked in those tight Levi's.

"You don't like horses much, do you?" she asked softly.

"I was hoping it didn't show," he said, his lips barely moving.

"Why did you come?" she wanted to know.

"Because I couldn't talk either of the others into it."

"You could have told us we couldn't ride."

"Devon, if I'd told you you couldn't ride, you'd have been shinnying down your balcony and over to these stables so fast it would have made my head spin."

She stopped her horse, and stared at him, outraged. "You knew!" she managed to splutter.

"Remarkable how you didn't worry about your skirt hitching up around your hips then," he noted easily.

She gasped. "You saw me leave? And you didn't stop me?"

"It's a free world, Devon. You're a free woman. You can go wherever you want to go. It's not my job to stop you, just to keep you safe."

"Well, you didn't do that particularly well, did you? What did you do? Say 'Aw, gee, she got away,' and then went and had your nap?'' Devon demanded.

"Not exactly. I said 'Aw, gee, she got away,' and then I said, 'Phil, go and watch that woman like a hawk,' and *then* I had a nap.''

"Nobody was following me,'' she told him triumphantly.

"As you already so shrewdly guessed, Miss Paige, we spend long hours training in sneakiness, in creeping through the woods without making a sound. Phil followed you every step of the way.''

"No, he didn't!''

Grey sighed. "You went off your balcony, dashed around the pool, across the lawn, and went into the woods at the path just east of the stables. You followed it to the rock outcropping that overlooks the house, where you had a rest, flagged your nose and said something to the effect of 'Carmichael, you incompetent creep'——''

"Clod,'' she corrected him tightly. "Did it amuse you to let me think I'd gotten away with it?''

"No, ma'am, I didn't find anything about that little incident very amusing.''

"Then why did you play me for a fool?''

"Who was playing whom for a fool?'' Grey asked sharply.

Devon was so humiliated and furious she briefly entertained the thought of hitting him. How dared he make her feel so small and stupid? Smacking him across the cheek, however, wouldn't hurt him nearly enough.

Instead, she jerked her horse around, dug her heels in and bounded away from him.

"Devon!"

She could hear the cold-blooded fury in his voice. She glanced over her shoulder. She had the better mount and the better riding skills, and she knew these trails like the back of her hand. He would never catch her. She was pulling away from him already.

Turning off on a trail that wasn't authorized on his silly little map, she headed, hell for leather, for home.

And then from somewhere behind her she heard a pained cry. She jerked her horse to a stop and twisted in her saddle. The path behind her was empty and still. She didn't hear a sound.

"Grey?" When there was no answer she pivoted the horse and went back down the path at a cautious trot.

And then she saw him, lying on the ground, still and twisted, the horse standing beside him.

Merciful God, what had she done? She had known he wasn't that great a horseman. How could she so thoughtlessly have presented him with a challenge that he would be honor bound not to refuse even if it was far above his skill level?

She yanked her horse to a stop in front of his inert body and vaulted from the saddle.

"Grey——" She crouched beside him, and reached out a tentative hand to touch the frightening stillness of his shoulder.

A hand snaked out and snared her ankle. She screamed with alarm, stood up and tried to twist her foot out of that iron grasp. Instead, she lost her balance and landed so hard on the packed ground that tears smarted in her eyes.

He let go of her ankle, and she used the split second to try and wriggle away, only to find herself pinned under the hard, lean length of his body and staring up into the shocking chill of harsh gray eyes.

"Don't . . . you . . . ever," he was saying, biting off each word, "try anything like that again."

She struggled impotently against his weight, and then lay gasping beneath him, furious and defiant. "What happened to 'it's a free world, Devon'? What happened to 'you're a free woman. You can go wherever you want to go'? What happened to all that?"

"Your privileges end where my job begins," he told her tersely. Mercifully, his weight shifted off her, but his fingers were like a biting steel handcuff around her wrist. He stood up, and unceremoniously jerked her to her feet.

"That was a rotten thing to do!" she said crossly, trying, ineffectually, to pry his fingers from around her wrist. "It was rotten to pretend you were hurt."

"Tough luck, princess, it got the job done."

"If you ever are really hurt," she said, giving up on his fingers and glaring at him, "don't look to me for help. Everybody knows about the little boy who cried wolf."

"I'm not the little boy," he told her dangerously, "I'm the wolf. And it isn't me who's in danger of being hurt. It isn't me whose name is penned in those letters. It isn't me who isn't showing an ounce—not one damned ounce—of sense. For God's sake, grow up, Devon!"

He released her wrist so suddenly, she staggered backward. She stood staring at him, rubbing her wrist, with tears stinging her eyes.

"Did I hurt you?" he asked, the anger draining from his voice.

"No," she said proudly, "you didn't. I'm ready to go now."

She turned back to her horse, but Grey was there before her. His hands spanned her waist and he tossed her easily up into the saddle. She held out her hand haughtily for the reins.

He just shook his head.

His meaning dawned on her. "If you think I'm going to be led around like a two-year-old on a pony, you're mistaken, Mr. Carmichael!" she snapped furiously.

"Sorry," he said. He led her horse over to where his was grazing by the side of the trail.

"Give me those reins, right now!"

"I rarely make the same mistake twice, incompetent clod that I am," he informed her, mounting his horse, his grip still firm on her reins.

"I won't do it again. You can trust me," she wheedled.

"Trust is earned," he told her patiently. "And when you've earned mine, we may try this little exercise again."

He pulled out in front of her and she stared helplessly at his broad, unyielding back. She felt extremely foolish. His tone, and even his technique, were not very different from what she used on her unruly five- and six-year-olds.

"Grey——" she began.

"I'm not discussing it further." He didn't even turn around and look at her.

"Well, I'm not going to be led into the yard like some escaped prisoner who's been rounded up by the posse!"

He stopped, twisted and looked at her. "If you don't like it this way, you always have the option of walking."

Her face mutinous, Devon slid off her horse and stood looking at him. This wasn't going to be much better—at least before the prisoner had been mounted. Now he could herd her in as if she was a renegade cow——

To her relief, he slid off his horse too. The barest trace of a smile took some of the frost out of his eyes. "I prefer walking," he informed her.

She felt as if she'd been double skunked!

Her riding boots were not designed for walking, and she was limping by the time they got back.

"Are you still planning to shop today?" he asked after escorting her to her bedroom door.

"Nothing on God's green earth could stop me," she told him through clenched teeth.

One thick eyebrow arched upward. "Really? What's the occasion?"

Revenge. "Oh, none," she said carelessly. "I just want to take full advantage of having someone to carry my bags."

The cool gray eyes scanned her face, and then he lifted one shoulder in a negligent shrug that told her he felt more than a match for anything she tried to throw at him.

"We'll just see about that," she muttered after she had slammed her bedroom door and limped painfully toward the shower.

"Look, Devon, you can put away the pretty pout," Grey informed her unsympathetically. "We are not going into L.A. in *that*."

"I'm not pouting. I just think you're being a little too militant about this whole thing." She watched him cross his arms over his chest, and knew, at once, that she had lost. *Again.* "Give me one good reason why we shouldn't take my car?"

"Partly because I dread the thought of you in control of this kind of horsepower," he muttered, "but mostly because a fire-engine-red Ferrari is just a little too conspicuous. Anyone looking for Devon Paige could spot you a mile off."

She supposed that made good sense, but it did present a problem. The clock was ticking. Monday, and her return to work after the spring break, was only a few days away, and there was no sign of whoever had been sending those letters being brought to justice. She was beginning to understand that she might warrant protection for a long, long time.

This was the only car she had. It was one of her few vanities. But thank goodness Grey had pointed out to her that it was a liability. She'd park it in the underground parking lot at her apartment and not use it for a while. It wouldn't cause her much hardship; she didn't drive her car to work anyway, though she often indulged herself after, unleashing all that power on the twisting coast roads of California.

Parking the car indefinitely would make it harder for *him* to find her. Mr. Carmichael had just made a mistake. It felt truly dreadful not to be able to tell him about it.

For an unsettling moment Devon almost wished she could be straight with him, and earn that trust he had talked about this morning. If there really were terrorists out there, writing letters with her name in them, he might be a reassuring fellow to have around. But that was impossible—simply impossible. One of the conditions of her being given the job at the school had been that the presence of Miss Devon Paige on the staff should not disrupt the routines of the school in any way. As in no reporters, as in no charity groups, headed by people who were her neighbors, taking a sudden interest in inner city schools. Of course, nobody had thought to mention bodyguards, but she was pretty sure that would be considered a disruption.

Besides, the price of having Grey's reassuring presence would be far too high. Because so far she had managed the impossible. She had managed to keep her father from disrupting her life. She was managing, slowly, to become normal, to do normal things, and enjoy normal pleasures. If Grey Carmichael found out where she worked, he would tell her father, and that would be the end of her freedom. Father was so paranoid. He just wouldn't be able to bear her working in the same neighborhood as streetwalkers, dope dealers and gangs. He wouldn't ever understand what her work meant to her, what it gave her.

She covertly studied Grey's strong profile as he ushered her over to an off white, nondescript sedan. She shivered. She didn't relish trying to give him the slip; she wasn't even sure she could. She felt his eyes resting, with question, on her face, and purposefully focused on the utilitarian interior of the car.

"Ugh!" she commented.

"It'll get us there, anonymously." The car purred to life, and Grey put it in gear.

"That's something I've never desired," she claimed, "anonymity." That wasn't true, but it was a good red herring. If Grey Carmichael believed she was a somewhat flashy, irresponsible and entirely selfish young woman, when the time came he would look for her in all the wrong places.

He would never guess how capable she was of deep caring, even altruism. He would never look for her in any of the places one might think of finding a "bleeding-heart liberal," as her father was given to calling her when she discussed with him her responsibility to herself and to the world, which was seldom.

"You're very quiet," Grey commented, his tone tinged with suspicion. The traffic was thickening as they approached Los Angeles.

"I don't always chatter like a monkey. And I don't *inflict* myself on people who don't appreciate me."

"It's not that I don't appreciate you," he said, flashing her one of those unexpected and completely wicked grins, "it's just that I feel I could appreciate you much, much more if you were somebody else's responsibility and I was hearing about your escapades secondhand."

It sounded suspiciously as if he might have forgiven her for this morning. She was not feeling nearly so big-hearted toward him.

She gave directions to a very exclusive boutique area, and made him leave the car in its parking lot. She made directly for a shop called "Women Only," which had a full display of lacy underthings in the window.

She gave him a smug smile. "If you'll wait here, I'll be back shortly," she told him.

To her severe annoyance, he didn't look at all taken aback. He looked amused. His cool gray eyes rested on the lacy display, and his mouth quirked slightly upward. "Doesn't look as if any of those packages you'll be wanting me to carry will be very heavy," he said dryly. He placed one big shoulder against the brick corner of the shop, folded his arms over his chest, and inclined his head mockingly at her. "Enjoy yourself," he said, not the least embarrassed.

Devon was furious. If he didn't have a knack for making her feel like a pigtailed schoolgirl with only the most juvenile sense of how to deal with an annoying man! So much for bringing him down to size— so much for dueling wits with him and winning! Now she was once again looking like an idiot child! She shoved her nose toward the heavens and marched into the store.

"You know," she said to the salesclerk who greeted her, "there's a very strange man hanging around your door."

Then she marched past her, and immersed herself in the deadly business of buying glamorous lingerie to replace the somewhat utilitarian cotton she had always preferred. The sexier it looked, the more it appealed. She tried on camisoles and teddies and string and lace, and outfits in innocent white and passionate red and velvety black. Her own reflection in the mirror came as a bit of a shock to her at first, but then she rather got into her own little fantasy. Also, knowing Grey was waiting out there gave her a great deal of satisfaction, and rather lent itself to the atmosphere of sexual fantasy she was creating.

"Are you finding everything you need?" the saleswoman asked.

"I certainly am."

"Oh, good, there they are now!" The woman turned to Devon. "I called the police on that rogue you mentioned outside the door. He didn't look like the perverted type, but all the same he *was* hanging around, and I couldn't imagine what kind of business he had doing that."

Devon's jaw dropped, and she threw on a silky black wrapper provided in the dressing room, and raced out into the main area of the store. She giggled nervously at what she saw. Grey was deep in conversation with the two police officers.

Unfortunately, he did not look the least perturbed by his predicament. She watched him produce a flat leather wallet, watched the respect straighten the shoulders of the two policeman as they saw what it contained. She turned back to the dressing room as she saw they were getting quite buddy-buddy.

"You can't come in here!" she heard the salesclerk gasping a few moments later. "This shop is exclusively——"

Devon peeked out of her changing-room. Grey flashed that same thin leather wallet at the saleslady, who responded by gasping like a fish and pointing directly at the changing rooms.

Devon slammed the dressing-room door and then bolted it. She waited, trembling.

In less than three seconds she heard the deep voice, just on the other side of her thin barrier.

"You get out here this minute, little miss, or I'll take the door off its hinges!"

"I'm not dressed," she squeaked.

"I don't care if you're buck naked, Devon. You get out here. I am about to read the riot act."

"I didn't know she'd call the police."

"One——" he began.

"Besides, you didn't get arrested——" A renegade chuckle slipped by her wary lips.

"Two——"

"And you made two new macho buddies who you can swill beer with on your days off——"

"Three."

Devon swiftly unlocked the door and stepped out in front of him in the skimpy black wrapper.

"I'm sorry," she said quickly and petulantly. His face was absolute cold stone—for a moment. And then his eyes traveled down the length of the wrapper, slowing on her long length of naked thigh, trailing down to her slender calf.

And then in half a stride he closed the remaining distance between them, curled his hand in the honeyed hair that hung down her back and forced her head back.

His lips descended on hers, angry and bruising. And even so, a slow heat stirred in the bottom of her belly, a sensation she had never experienced before. And instead of struggling from the punishing ferocity of his lips, she found herself melting into the white-hot heat of his anger, and then tentatively, ever so tentatively, meeting it, feeling anger recede, to be replaced by something even hotter.

She stood on tiptoe, pressed her softness into the hard wall of his chest, released, without even knowing it, some of the restraint that had held her captive all the days of her life. She swayed as the heat moved to her legs, drugged her being, sucked her very ability to control her muscles from her.

Without warning, Grey pulled away, though his hands remained curled into her shoulders so she wouldn't slump forward again.

She stared at him with dazed eyes, then touched her tingling lips. She pulled back from him.

He seemed to land back on earth with a thump. He let go of her shoulders abruptly, and shoved his short hair back from his brow. "That should never have happened," he said tonelessly.

Her voice was lost. If she could have found it she might have said something sarcastic such as, wasn't that how he'd threatened to deal with a difficult woman right from the beginning? But remembering that left her feeling bereft, where a moment ago there had been vibrancy dancing within her.

"It won't happen again," he said with tight and intimidating professionalism. "My apologies, Miss Paige. I was out of line—way out of line."

The way he said it would never happen again, as if he was going to place all his power, and he was a powerful man, behind that particular objective, should have made her feel very safe. Instead, some devil within her wanted to make him break his vow within seconds of having made it.

But he turned and walked rapidly away from her. He passed the gap-mouthed clerk with a casual nod of his head.

And as soon as he was gone Devon felt his power over her diminish. Was she insane? She'd actually contemplated seducing a man in the middle of a public shop? She who had never seduced anybody, anywhere?

She closed the dressing-room door and leaned on it. So much for striking a resounding chord for all sisterhood, she thought. She'd succumbed to his charms with less confrontation than the flower-loving Ferdinand the Bull had given the matadors!

Grey's mocking warning of that first day came back to haunt her. "If," he had told her, "in some moment of incomprehensible madness, I ever decided to kiss you, the last thing on your mind would be biting my nose.''

Absolutely the last thing, she agreed with a defeated sigh. What on earth had happened? What had brought on that moment he had so aptly predicted as incomprehensible madness?

Damn it, there *was* something fiercely compelling about him. What was the point of trying to deny the fact? The world would still be round, even if she claimed it was flat a million and one times. Grey Carmichael would still possess an animal magnetism, an enticing virility, a forceful masculinity even if she tried to focus on the more aggravating sides of his nature—of which there were many, she reminded herself.

She didn't like the man! In two days he had outwitted her, embarrassed her, humiliated her and made her feel small, stupid, insensitive and childish.

And more like a woman than she had ever felt.

In a few days, she reminded herself, it would be over. She knew, suddenly, that she would succeed in getting away from him, because she had to. She was not accustomed to turmoil, to stress, to tension. That was what had brought on this ridiculous episode, his presence stirring up her life and her emotions as if they were so much fruit and yogurt.

What was he doing to her? It was true she had always had a mischievous streak, and always been a high-spirited young woman, but those qualities had always been tempered with her other attributes. Her colleagues would be shocked to see quiet, mature, dedicated Devon Paige behaving as she had the last little while.

It was probably something biological, she concluded, and she had better make good her escape before she turned into one giant hormone.

She paid for her things abstractedly. First, she would have to figure out how to get out of the house. That would be the only hard part. And maybe not so hard. Grey had to sleep some time, and Michael Wilson was definitely a weak link in the chain.

And if there were really terrorists? Well, they certainly wouldn't be looking for a society girl like Miss Devon Paige in the classroom of an inner city school!

It wasn't until she got in the car that she thought to ask herself why on earth she'd purchased every single item she'd tried on.

CHAPTER FOUR

"WHAT exactly does a night maid do?" Mike Wilson asked innocently.

Grey Carmichael's bacon-laden fork froze halfway up to his mouth. His instincts rarely let him down, and red warning lights were flashing in his brain. He cautioned himself not to rattle the kid. "A night maid?" he asked, his tone more lethal than he'd intended.

"Well, last night, around midnight, I was making my rounds and there was an old gal letting herself out the front door. 'Sorry if I startled you, sir,' she said, 'just the night maid going off duty.' It's been nagging me ever since. What does a night maid do? Place freshly heated rocks at the bottom of the beds?" He started to laugh in enjoyment of his own humor, but when he saw Grey wasn't joining him his laughter caught in his throat.

"You did ask to see her credentials, of course?" But Grey asked the question sinkingly. He was already getting up, tossing down his napkin.

"Er—no, but I knew her. I mean, not her name or anything, but she looked familiar to me."

Grey reached for the two-way radio on the sideboard, and gave Mike a withering look. "I'll bet she looked familiar to you!" He spoke into the radio. "Moriarty, you there? Check the garage—now!" He put down the radio, raced out of the room and took the stairs three at a time. He burst through the door of Devon's room without knocking. There was no reason to knock on the door of a room he was one hundred percent sure was empty.

He spared Wilson, who came in behind him and was staring, his face pale, at the empty, unmade bed, one caustic glance. "Gee," he said brutally, "it looks like the night maid missed a bed."

"Oh, God, Grey," the young man said softly, "I'm sorry. It was late, and everything was peaceful, and I was a bit tired. I never even thought——"

"Yeah. Well, people who forget to think on this job usually end up dead. Or getting someone else killed."

"She was wearing a gray wig or something. And she had on granny glasses and this frumpy dress. Even you wouldn't have known——"

"Did you read the file I gave you on her?" Grey asked cuttingly.

"Yes, but——"

"Don't 'yes-but' me! She took drama options all through university. Do you think maybe she knew a thing about costumes, makeup, *acting*? On the very first day we were in here, she took off. You should have been on red alert from that moment on. Night maid! I guess we better count ourselves lucky that she didn't manage to sell you a bridge before she got out the door."

"Do you think Miss Paige is in danger?" Wilson asked in a small voice.

Grey measured the very real distress in the young man's face, and sighed inwardly, though he didn't let a hint of sympathy cross his features. Wilson wasn't stupid; he was just unseasoned. He didn't yet wear wariness and suspicion like a second skin. His mind didn't race ahead yet, exploring every possibility, every angle. He was still human. He still trusted.

He probably had the potential to be good at this job some day.

"She's in danger," he said, his voice deliberately harsh. To himself he added, of being on the receiving end of a damn good licking from me. But he offered no such reassurance to Mike Wilson. The kid had to start learning to treat every situation as real, not a practice run. If he didn't he would end up dead. It was that easy—and that hard. That ruthlessly, depressingly hard. Grey turned away from Wilson's expression, that pleaded for forgiveness and understanding.

"Go call the Colonel," he snapped. Resignedly, he began to open desk drawers. Somewhere in here there would be a clue to where Devon had gone. And he would find it. And her.

"The Ferrari's gone," Moriarty offered from the doorway.

Grey sifted through some papers. "Wilson's greener than the grass over the septic tank, Phil, but what's your excuse?"

"I don't have one, Grey. She gave me the keys to her car yesterday afternoon and told me her friend Bonnie would be by to pick it up. She told me that somebody might as well be getting some use out of it, since you weren't going to allow her to use it. All I thought at the time was, geez, I wish I had a friend who'd like to see me using their Ferrari for a week or two.

"I accept full culpability for the fact that she got off the grounds without my being aware of it."

Grey gave Phil a brief look of appreciation. Good man, he thought. No excuses. Phil gave him a look of sympathy. They both knew that as senior man in the house Grey would take the flak for the foul-up, no matter who owned up to being responsible.

"The Colonel wants to speak to you." A very subdued Mike Wilson returned to the room.

Grey picked up the telephone extension, turned his back on his co-workers, and steeled himself for what he knew had to come.

"What the hell happened there, Carmichael?" demanded the Colonel.

"It appears we've been given the slip, sir."

"I know that much! I want to know how!"

"I don't know that yet, sir. It wasn't my watch."

"Is that an excuse, Carmichael?"

Grey managed to catch the sigh before it became audible. "No, sir."

Grey listened unflinchingly to a very colorful blast of ill temper and outrage.

"... and you're one of the most experienced men in one of the most respected law enforcement agencies in the world. And a *girl* outwitted you..."

Grey decided not to point out to the Colonel that his remark was decidedly sexist. Devon Paige was no *girl*.

"I don't care whose shift it was. If she got away that clean, she *planned* on leaving, and you should have caught something. A change in attitude, tension—*something*!"

There had been both, Grey acknowledged uncomfortably. But they'd been in him too, and they'd been a result of that disturbing, devastating meeting of lips. The Colonel was absolutely right. He should have caught it, should have been set on guard by her change of mood, her false cheer, her agreeableness, the edginess that had underrun both. But he'd broken the rules—lost, for a flash, the incisive profession-alism that gave him his edge. And a flash was all it took, as he had just so sanctimoniously informed Mike Wilson.

"...and you'll be celebrating your eighty-second birthday in the Colombian jungle if you don't have her back within the day, Mr. Carmichael!"

Grey bit the inside of his cheek. "Yes, sir."

"I didn't hear you, Mr. Carmichael."

He bit harder, and the silence lengthened between them. He wished the Colonel had stayed with the Marines. He wished *he'd* stayed with the Marines. He wished he'd never been assigned to an enigma like Devon Paige with her biting wit, strangely soft eyes, and her subtly sensuous lips.

"Yes, sir," he repeated, marginally louder. The Colonel hung up. Grey gently replaced the dead re-ceiver, and took a deep breath. He turned back to the room, ignoring the looks of sympathy from Wilson and Moriarty.

"Moriarty, get the police to issue an APB. Wilson, start going through this room," he ordered.

Wilson, eager to please, flung open the nearest drawer—and blanched. "I don't think anything in here——"

Grey felt the oddest ripple go through him when he realized that Mike had stumbled into her lingerie drawer. He didn't want the kid going through her most intimate things. He didn't want anybody doing that. It seemed like a violation of the worst sort, a viola-tion of those eyes. But he'd already lost his edge to those eyes once, and he couldn't afford to do it again. He knew darn well where women tucked away their secrets.

Grey steeled himself. She'd lost her right to privacy when she'd waltzed out of that door.

"Search the room," he said coldly. *"Carefully."* Grimly, he went out of the door to wake up Mr. Paige. He'd probably have some idea where his daughter would go.

Ten minutes later he had the full picture of how little Mr. Paige knew about his daughter—and why. He actually understood her a little bit—her hostility, her fierce independence—for the first time.

At any other time he might have actually appreciated her fervent struggle for freedom from the well-meant but ultimately suffocating indulgence of her father. But all he could think of now was how hard it was going to be to find somebody who had become so practiced at hiding her tracks.

Inside one day.

Mike Wilson appeared. "There wasn't anything in her drawers." He blushed bright red at his inadvertent pun.

"Okay." Grey pulled on his jacket. "Start calling her friends and acquaintances. I'll call back on the hour."

Devon was exhausted, and happy. She sat cross-legged, in a circle of children, the children on either side practically in her lap, they were cuddling so closely.

"A," she sang out, "stands for alligators." She bared her teeth and growled, and the children laughed lovingly, their eyes riveted on her face. "Your turn, Francie."

"B is for ... belly," the little corn-braided girl next to her sang tunelessly, then pulled up her shirt to display her belly button and chuckled joyously.

I belong here, Devon thought, squeezing Francie's hand approvingly. She'd had her doubts about the wisdom of what she was doing several times last night and this morning, but as soon as she'd seen the faces of her children she knew she'd done exactly right. They needed her.

And she needed them. Somehow she felt different here, among them. Real. It was the only time she ever felt real. Everywhere else it was as if she was playing a role, always trying to figure out what was expected of her and then be that. But here, in faded jeans, with her hair in a simple braid running down her back, and no makeup on, and her hand caught rather ferociously in grubby little grips, she felt in touch with herself, her soul.

Alfonso slipped in at the door, and she grinned a welcome at him, and was rewarded when a smile lightened the perpetual sullen look on his face. Alfonso had been sentenced to do some community work after being caught in an act of vandalism in his apartment building. His sentence had been up months ago, and yet he kept coming back, looking desperately and pathetically for a place to belong, other than those cold, hard streets.

The cold, hard streets these innocent children walked in from, hungry, physically hungry, and emotionally starved. And Devon believed if she could just love them enough maybe it would change the course of their fates just a little bit.

"Could I do the closing?" he asked, and slipped into the circle.

"Thanks, Alfonso."

"Sure," he said, making a bad attempt at hiding his eagerness. "Okay, everybody, one best thing and one worst thing that happened today."

Devon slipped out of the circle. She almost always joined in, liking it as much as the children and Alfonso. But today she was so tired. She'd been up late for several nights, watching Phil's security routine outside until she was sure of it, sure of the exact moment he went around the back of the house, and sure of exactly how long it took him to check the grounds behind the house and then reappear at the front. Just long enough for her to race across the open stretch of lawn into the bushes, and make her way cross-country to where Bonnie had left her car for her.

She grinned with remembrance. Making it past Mike Wilson had definitely been the best part. He hadn't even suspected. Her humor left her. The poor kid had probably been bawled out royally by Grey Carmichael!

Her kindergarten class was ready to go now, and it took several more minutes to bestow hugs and kisses on each and to listen to several secrets.

"I came to give you a message from Mr. Peters," Alfonso remembered. "You're getting a classroom aide tomorrow."

Mr. Peters was the principal. Devon was astonished. She had forty-three children in her classroom, some of them hopelessly behind, and she had requested an aide more than once. But the money situation was incredibly tight in the school system, and she was surprised to be having her request granted now.

She glanced at the clock. Her class was let out an hour before the others. Mr. Peters would be teaching maths at the moment. Any other day, she would be in the school for at least another hour, doing lesson plans, marking and thinking of new and innovative ways to hold her pupils' attention for ten or fifteen minutes. But today exhaustion was catching up with her.

"Would you tell him I won't be able to talk to him about it until tomorrow? First thing?" she said.

"Sure. Does this mean you won't want me to help you any more?"

She was somewhat taken aback by the almost feral expression of hostility on Alfonso's face. "Of course that's not what it means," she said as gently as possible. "It just means we'll be able to do so much more with the children." She slung her bag over her shoulder. "See you tomorrow."

"Want me to walk you to the bus stop?" queried Alfonso.

"I'll be fine."

"I better walk you."

She shrugged, and they walked out into the muggy heat together. She paused on the school steps, and got an uneasy sensation, the hair rising on the back of her neck.

Somebody's watching me, she thought. She scanned the crowded streets. The tempo of the street was lively and colorful, but not a single soul seemed to have even noticed her.

Giving Alfonso a little wave, she boarded her bus a few minutes later, but the feeling of uneasiness did not leave her. And because she was so tired, her imagination began to work overtime.

What if there really were terrorists? What if somebody had watched her leave the school and had climbed on the bus with her? What if she was being stalked, slowly and thoroughly? Just half an hour ago she had still been pleased with her evasion of her security team in general, and Grey in particular. What if that had been the most foolish move of her entire life?

She looked warily around the bus, and felt relieved. Again, nobody was the least bit interested in her. And again her uneasiness did not go away.

When she had to get off the bus she did so nervously, watching who got off at the same stop as her. Several people did, but none of them even looked remotely like terrorists, or anyone who would do her harm.

Good guys and bad guys look remarkably alike.

Devon walked briskly through her pleasant middle-income neighborhood. One of the people who had been on the bus walked behind her—a man. She slowed her pace. His slowed too. He didn't attempt to pass her.

With her heart thudding she practically ran up the steps to her apartment building, wrestled with the key until the sweat actually beaded on her forehead, then plummeted through the door when it unexpectedly opened. She flung her back against it and, gasping like a fish, peered out through the glass. The street was empty. She pressed her nose against the window. Her "terrorist" had continued up the block and was crossing the street.

Her nerves still tingling and her heart still racing, she took the lift to the third floor and her own modest little apartment.

She opened the door to the blackness of the hallway. A feeling of relief and safety enveloped her, and she closed the door behind her.

A hand circled her neck, and clamped tightly over her mouth.

"Hello, Devon," a voice growled in her ear.

She recognized the voice. No, even before the voice she had recognized the aroma of him, and the fear that had been balled like a hard fist in her stomach melted into a feeling of safety such as she had never known. Of course, she could never let him see she was somewhat relieved her little game had not worked out. That would be a defeat of the most humiliating kind.

His hand slid away from her mouth and his arm from around her neck. She whirled and glared at him, her hands on her slender hips.

She was confronted with six feet two inches of coldly angry Grey Carmichael.

"What do you think you're doing?" she demanded. "I could have had a heart attack!"

"I'm trying to instil the fear of God into you," he informed her unrepentantly. "It could just as easily be a terrorist standing here as me, and then, my dear Miss Paige, a heart attack would be the least of your problems."

Devon marched, head high, down the hall. She went into her sunny kitchen and opened the fridge and poured herself a glass of fruit juice. "How did you find me?" she demanded. "And if you say it's your job, I think I'll scream!"

He was regarding her silently and gravely. "I found you the same way any self-respecting terrorist would find you. I traced you through the California Teachers' Association."

She nearly choked on her orange juice. "Those files are confidential!"

"Nothing's confidential, Devon."

"Do you mean you bought somebody?" she said with disgust.

"It's not even that hard. People give away information they have no business giving away all the time. You just have to know how to ask for it."

She glared at him. Oh, and he'd know how to ask for it. He'd turn all that macho charm on some poor unsuspecting bored-out-of-her-mind clerk, and she'd unwittingly babble state secrets to win the flash of those white teeth and the warmth of those smoky gray eyes.

"How did you get in my apartment?" she went on. "I bet you did something tacky—and illegal—like picking the lock with a credit card."

"I don't know how to pick locks with credit cards. If you do, I wouldn't mind a lesson. I told your landlady I was your cousin from Des Moines and that you'd told me you'd leave me a key, but must have forgotten."

His lethal charm hard at work again.

"You could have waited outside instead of skulking around in the dark waiting to scare me half to death," Devon pointed out.

"I just wanted to get the lie of the land." She heard a note of something almost like guilt in his voice. "As for scaring you half to death, I apologize. Mary told me you always arrived home at precisely five. You're nearly an hour early."

"Mary?" she queried.

"Your landlady."

"Funny, I've lived here for nearly two years and I've never been invited to call her anything but Mrs. Simpson-Wells."

Grey spread his palms before her as if to say it was a gift some were born with—and she was not one of them.

"I hope I didn't get Michael and Phil into trouble," she added.

"That's very altruistic of you! Maybe if you didn't want to get them into trouble, you should have used your common sense and stayed put."

"Did *you* get in trouble?" she asked with deliberate relish.

He leaned one of his shoulders against the wall and hooked his thumbs through his belt loops, his eyes still resting on her face. "Yeah. Does that make you happy?"

Oddly enough, it didn't, though she wasn't about to let him in on that.

"So what now?" she queried.

"Devon, I want you to understand something. You could be in grave danger. This was a very foolish stunt. Don't try anything like it again."

She tossed her head, despite the fact that a shiver of pure fear had raced up her spine. "As a matter of fact, I don't have any secrets left," she shrugged.

"Couldn't you have just told me?" he asked in a pained growl, and suddenly she was aware that he'd been *worried*. His relief wasn't because he had an angry boss waiting in the wings, it was because he'd been genuinely concerned about her. For a reason she did not want to contemplate, that made her heart beat a fraction more swiftly, and brought a warm glow to the bottom of her stomach.

"I thought you'd probably tell dear old Dad where I lived and worked, and that would be the end of everything I've tried to achieve over the last two years," she explained.

"All you had to do was ask me not to."

She gave him a skeptical look. "And you wouldn't have?"

"I don't report to your father. And after my talk with him after your disappearance I can even understand why you feel so driven to rebellion. But, Devon, I'm not on his payroll, and it really is your safety that's my concern. I'm not going to do anything to impinge on your private life."

"You already have, Grey," she said softly. Among other things, her life was changed simply because he was here in her sanctuary, his powerful presence made it seem small and cramped, like a playhouse.

"What I meant was I'm not trying to change you or your life-style," he explained. "Nothing I do will have any kind of permanent effect on your life."

As if one could ever forget eyes that looked like that, she thought.

"Okay, okay," she said wearily, "I give up. I surrender."

"Devon, I brought copies of several of those threatening letters to show you. I didn't want to do that, but you have to grasp the situation. It's important—especially now—that you cooperate with me."

"Why especially now?" she queried.

Wordlessly Grey reached into his inside suit pocket, and handed her several folded photocopies.

Taking her fruit juice in one hand and the letters in the other, she brushed by him, and curled up in one corner of the pastel-colored love seat that served as a couch in the tiny one-person apartment. It was a comfortable room, casual as opposed to opulent.

Her eyes widened as she read the first letter. "My gosh, vulgar doesn't begin to say it, does it?"

She read the second one swiftly, felt a shiver go down her spine, and held them out to Grey. "I can't say I can make much sense out of them. They seem to be gibberish. Though I must say, I find it disturbing seeing my name in that awful scrawl."

"That's one of the reasons we decided against showing you the notes," he explained. "Nobody wanted you to be any more disturbed than you had to be."

"In other words," she said, a touch wryly, "nobody wanted a panicky woman on their hands."

He shrugged. "You were an unknown quantity at the time."

"My heart is warmed by the fact you now trust me not to panic," she said dryly.

"Actually, I'm more interested in scaring the dickens out of you. I'd rather cope with panic than escape attempts," he confessed, "particularly successful ones. I want you to look at how those are signed."

Devon glanced down at them. "Is that supposed to mean something to me?"

"I find it a disturbing coincidence that those letters are signed 'Heart of the Ghetto,' and you're working smack-dab in the middle of the inner city."

She felt the blood drain from her face, and she knew he'd done exactly what he'd set out to do. It was finally coming home that this was not a game.

"Somebody was watching me when I left school today," she told him. "I could feel it."

Grey nodded. "One of ours. But pay attention to those feelings, Devon." He sighed. "I have a confession to make."

"What's that?"

"I searched your place."

"For what?" she asked, amazed.

"I was hoping to find just one hint of illegal activity—a little dope in an ashtray or something."

"I don't indulge," she said stiffly. "I hardly ever drink a bottle of beer, for heaven's sake!"

"I think I was aware of that before I started looking," he admitted.

"So why did you look?"

"Because I was angry enough to think it would be just the right thing to get you arrested and put in a nice safe jail somewhere for a few days until all this blows over."

"You wouldn't dare!" she huffed.

"It was just a passing fancy, but I wouldn't advise making me that angry again, Devon."

"Yes, sir," she said snippily.

"Oh, and one other thing," he added. "I pulled a few strings, and you have a new aide starting in your classroom tomorrow."

"I knew it was too good to be true."

"We're going to say I'm an adult student at UCLA——"

"Nobody's ever going to believe *you* are a teacher's aide!"

"—completing my degree before I start teaching physical education."

"To the Green Beret?" she asked sarcastically. "How many times did you have to promise to wine and dine the clerk at the Teachers' Association to pull off all this?"

"Twice." He said it so deadpan she couldn't tell if he was serious or not.

But she became very serious. "Grey, don't do anything to jeopardize my job. It means the world to me. I was told when I was hired that my presence in the school was not to cause any disruptions. Somehow I think having a bodyguard in my classroom might classify as that, don't you?"

"Maybe you should trust people who care about you enough that this kind of disruption isn't what was meant by that clause in your contract at all," he told her.

"I don't want to take the chance of finding out."

"I feel I should at least tell your principal."

"No!" she said forcefully.

"Okay, Devon, we'll play it your way, for now. But this is the deal—I won't do anything to jeopardize the way you perform your job, and you won't do anything to jeopardize the way I perform mine."

Devon nodded. He was being more than fair, considering what she had just put him through. She felt satisfied. Her feeling lasted all of three seconds.

"Where are you going to stay, Grey?" she asked him.

"Here."

"Here?" That was utterly impossible. This wasn't Redwoods, where she could give him a choice of bedrooms. He could sleep on the couch—but only if he thought he'd be comfortable in the jackknife position. No, he couldn't anyway. He couldn't sleep on her couch. And share her bathroom with her. And her shower. And her fridge. She'd be bumping into him all the time. She'd be fighting with him over which TV show to watch. She'd be cooking him supper!

In time, if he was that damned close all the time, she might start thinking, again, of what his lips tasted like.

"You cannot stay here."

"Where would you like me to stay? The Hilton? It's only a few miles away. I could call now and then and see how you're doing."

"Oh, do what they do on TV. Don't they sit in their cars and swill coffee or something?" She softened her tone. "You can't stay here, Grey. Look at this place! It was built for one small person. How could you stay in here with me and not impinge on my privacy?"

He rocked on his heels for a minute. "I could probably get use of a safe house close to here."

"No, Grey." She didn't want to be under the same roof as him, that was all. Within her was an old-fashioned sense of propriety, not to mention a well-honed sense of self-preservation.

"Okay," he said resignedly. "I'll have to work out something else."

"Right."

After making a few phone calls and giving her enough security instructions to run Sing-Sing single-handedly, he left her. Devon flopped down on her little couch and went fast asleep.

She got up in the night to go to bed, and peered carefully out her window. She could see Grey sitting in his car in front of the building, and felt a little

twinge of compassion for him, before she shuffled off
to bed.

Grey came into her classroom with Mr. Peters the next
morning. When they were introduced she carefully
pretended she had never met him, though she couldn't
help but notice his face held lines of incredible weariness in it.

Alfonso had glued himself to a book cabinet as soon
as the stranger entered the room, but she brought Grey
over to him. Alfonso's eyes, street-hard and wary,
fastened on Grey.

"This is Mr. Carmichael." The young man looked
as if he was going to scurry out of the door. Instead
he jammed his hands into his pockets and regarded
Grey sullenly.

Devon glanced up into Grey's features and immediately understood why Alfonso was being defensive.
Grey's eyes were as wary and watchful as Alfonso's—
only there was sternness and strength in his steady
unflinching gaze.

"Grey's going to be helping in the classroom for a
while, Alfonso," she told him.

She saw the instant jealousy in his face and then
the narrowing of those slanted eyes.

"You ain't no classroom helper," Alfonso muttered in the direction of Grey's shoe.

"That's right," Grey responded, his voice low and
calm, almost casual. But his eyes fastened on Alfonso
with—challenge?

Alfonso ducked his head and went out of the door.

Devon glared at Grey. "You promised you wouldn't
jeopardize my position here. You practically told him
who you were!"

"You play a lot of hunches in this business," Grey said unapologetically.

"Alfonso is a nice young man, Grey, despite appearances. There was no need to look at him as though he was a criminal—he's defensive enough."

Grey looked at her with something like amusement. "Careful, Mama Hen, that you don't have a cobra among your chicks."

"What does that mean?"

He shrugged. "I didn't get a good feeling from him. It may be nothing."

"It *is* nothing," she insisted hotly, and sketched Alfonso's history for him, especially emphasizing the nobility of his staying on after his sentence was over.

"Gee," Grey said dryly, "I'm sure sorry I looked at him as though he were a criminal."

"Oh! I'm trying to make the point that he doesn't have to wear that brand for the rest of his life. That he's making an honest effort at rehabilitating himself. You," she said emphatically, "are not going to get along with these kids."

But, amazingly enough, he did. He fitted smoothly into her routine, aside from the fact that she felt rather self-conscious with him in the room, seeing her for the first time in her most flattering light, at what she did best. And the children seemed to like and accept him immediately.

She commented to him about that when the children had all gone home for the day.

"I like kids," Grey said, "I like them a lot. I think they probably just sensed that, and needed to be given some male attention."

"If you like kids so much," she turned away from him, and busied herself cleaning the board, "why don't you get married and have some?"

The silence behind her was unnerving. She finally turned and looked at him.

"This job isn't very conducive to conducting a successful relationship."

She suspected he was speaking from experience. "Does that make you unhappy?" she asked.

"Sometimes."

His eyes were resting on her face. He still looked tired enough to drop. And she supposed maybe it was because of that that she caught a glimpse behind his impassive mask. For an instant, in the grayness of his eyes, she saw immense loneliness, like a prairie landscape in winter with a wind howling across it.

"Oh, Grey," she said softly, "when you meet the right woman it won't matter to her what you do." She didn't even realize she was unconsciously leaning toward him until he stepped back.

His mask had snapped back into place. "Yeah, right," he said cynically.

She felt foolish for presuming to give a man who no doubt had a wealth of experience with women any kind of advice.

"Of course," she said icily, "you'd probably have to give up floozy blondes and Russian spies."

"In that case, I'm not interested," he came back dryly. He glanced at his watch. "Do you think we could go? I'm being relieved for a few hours so I can get some sleep."

Half an hour later Devon was home, and introduced to the new agent, who would watch her premises from the car and make occasional checks of the building and hallway, just as Grey had done last night.

Grey went over all the security precautions, *again*. Even though that annoyed her, she felt the strangest sensation when he walked away.

For just an instant a wind, bleak as a prairie landscape in winter, howled across her heart.

CHAPTER FIVE

"I'M GOING to have a few friends in tomorrow night for dinner and cards," Devon announced to Grey, after school the following day. Never let it be said that she was one of those people who didn't know how to cope with loneliness.

Never let it be said that she would even fleetingly entertain such wild and unsubstantiated notions as the solution for *her* loneliness lurking somewhere in the depths of *his* gray eyes.

"Fine. If you could give me a list of the names of people you intend to ask, I'll try to have a security check run. Next time, I'd appreciate a few more days' notice."

She hardly knew which of those issues to address first! She had noticed that Grey seemed irritable and preoccupied today, and she had no intention of suffering at the whim of his bad mood.

"I trust my friends, and you're insulting both me and them by saying you're going to run a security check. I won't have it!" she said angrily.

"Then what you won't be having is a dinner party." He said this calmly, with the aggravating authority of a man far too accustomed to having the last word in these things.

She folded her arms stubbornly over her chest. "I don't see how you can stop me! I'll invite people, and they'll come, and short of putting a barricade around the building——"

"Devon, I appreciate your loyalty to your friends. As a friend, it's your job to trust them. Unfortunately, it's my job not to trust anybody. A security check is done fairly quietly. They won't even know one has been conducted." Grey looked at her thoughtfully. "I thought we were going to try and cooperate with one another?"

"You said my life wasn't going to be disrupted. What a joke! I can't even be spontaneous with my friends. In other words, I seem to be the one who does all the cooperating and compromising!"

"Is that right? I haven't noticed you spending eight hours in a car yet." For the first time, a hint of anger entered his voice.

Somewhat chastened, Devon tore a sheet of paper from a notebook and wrote the names of her friends on it. She wished he hadn't mentioned the car. She'd noticed he was back in it this morning when she got up, and wondered, just a shade guiltily, if that was why he was so irritable today. She couldn't think of anything she would hate doing more than spending eight hours in a car watching someone's darkened apartment window.

"Thank you," he said levelly when she shoved the note at him.

"What do you do for eight hours in the car?" she asked. "Read?"

"No, ma'am. I turn on the radio, very low, and I watch and I listen."

"For eight hours?" she asked incredulously. "No wonder you're crabby!"

"At least I have an excuse for my disposition."

"I have one too. I was in a good mood until you started snapping out orders about *my* dinner party. It makes me feel like a prisoner."

He sighed. "Devon, I'm sorry I wasn't the soul of diplomacy. You're right, I'm out of sorts today. And it doesn't have much to do with sitting in that car."

"You hate this assignment, don't you?" she accused.

"It's not that I hate it," he said slowly. "I just feel my talents would be of better use someplace else right now. Don't take that personally."

"As if I would!"

"I think you take a lot more personally than you let on."

"Well, I don't," she said, a touch shrilly.

"Fine," he said dryly. "Forget I mentioned it."

"I will." But she didn't.

It was nice having people in on Thursday night. Devon invited her friend Bonnie, two young men who were friends from their university days, a teacher from school, and his wife. They ate lasagne, then played Trivial Pursuit afterward. It felt wonderful to laugh and play, and pretend everything was normal. But no matter how hard she tried she couldn't quite forget that Grey was out there in his car, alone and probably bored out of his mind while she was having fun.

She wondered, once, glancing out of the window at that familiar nondescript sedan, as she went into the kitchen to get more Coke, what he would have said if she had invited him to come.

He would probably have said yes. For security reasons.

And he would probably have had her friends eating out of the palm of his hand in seconds. Dave, from school, already knew Grey and liked him. Everybody at school liked him. Her dire predictions that he would never be able to pass himself off as a teacher's aide had proved entirely wrong.

He was obviously adept at passing himself off as any number of things, she had noted cynically, as she had watched him get into his role as a teacher's helper. He dressed the part, wearing the classic university uniform of faded jeans and casual sport shirts extremely well. That particular mode of dress showed off the hard-muscled lines of his body to best advantage, and no one would have ever thought to question the fact that he was a physical education major.

With the children he was actually *playful*. He told stories vividly laced with atrocious faces and a huge repertoire of voices. He listened so attentively to the tales told to him, laughed with such a genuine appreciation, casually roughed heads, generously squeezed little hunched shoulders and little sweaty hands.

In the staff room he was also a hit. The women, it seemed to Devon, were all subtly jockeying for position during coffee and lunch. A veritable crowd seemed to form around Grey, leaving Devon munching, miffed, by herself on the other side of the room. He was just so damned charming! From her vantage point away from the crowd she cynically noticed his wiliness. What everybody thought was charm was really his ability to get the conversation away from himself. Queries about him were usually answered with one vague phrase, and then he'd turn the full blast of his charm on his inquisitor. "And what about you? Where did you go to school? Really? Great ball team... I'll bet you worked on the paper..."

The wretched man spoke six languages. He was well versed on everything from the theory of relativity to how fast the log ride at Disneyland actually moved. Well, let him charm them all. Let them jockey for seats around him. Devon *knew* the truth. He would talk about anything only so that he never had to talk about himself. He could turn any conversation that looked, even vaguely, as if it might be heading for the sacred secrets that it was part of his job to protect.

She turned away from the window. She was glad she hadn't invited him! As if she needed to be around him any more than she already was! Why had such a strange and silly thought even crossed her mind? To spend a social evening with Grey? Ridiculous!

The party broke up early as everyone was working the next day. A few minutes after her guests had departed a soft knock sounded on her door. Thinking someone had forgotten something, she flung it back open.

Grey stood there. "You're supposed to ask who it is," he reminded her, his voice rough, his face forbidding.

"I thought it was one of my——"

"I don't want to hear excuses."

She stared at him. The harshness in his voice seemed rather out of proportion to the crime.

"I just forgot," she said defensively.

"Look, Devon—I'm tired of it. I'm tired of your forgetting, and bucking me at every turn, and refusing to take anything seriously. From now on, I'm doing my job and that's it. No extras, no reminders, no reprimands. You take some responsibility for yourself too, because I'm not doing it all."

Her mouth fell open, and she closed it with a snap. She actually felt a sneaky little tear smarting behind her eye. What had she done to deserve this?

"I'd like to look around," Grey told her.

"None of my friends left bombs here," she told him with far more fierceness than was necessary.

He gave her a disgusted look, as if his little lecture had been wasted on an idiot, then shoved past her, and did a quick tour of her premises.

Devon watched him, still smarting from his sharpness. What was wrong with him tonight? His sternness was usually laced with an underlying dry humor. She had never seen him look quite so remote, quite so cold, quite so professional and at the same time removed and uncaring.

He finished looking around and brushed by her.

"Good night, Miss Paige."

She closed the door behind him. She knew he usually waited in the hall until he heard her put the chain lock over the door. Tonight she could hear his footsteps retreating before that.

The encounter left her feeling agitated. She did some straightening up, then turned on the news.

The lead item was about a drug bust gone wrong. The shipment had come from Colombia. One agent was in critical condition, another wounded, but not as severely.

Grey's edginess today was suddenly not only explainable but understandable. He would have known this was happening today. He would have been waiting for news, and when he got it, it was bad. His harshness outside her door was not so much directed at her; it was the wounded voice of a man who had seen too much violence, who knew its reality, and saw her as careless because she did not know that same reality.

Grey's friends, she thought. His operation—the one he had had to miss because of this assignment.

Why did she feel washed over and over again with relief? After all, if he'd been there, instead of here, she would never have known him in the first place. He would have been just a name on the news. Still, she was glad he was here, safe, out in that car, no matter how bitter and angry he felt about it.

She went and put on her pajamas and brushed out her hair. She turned out all the lights, then was drawn like a magnet to her window. She looked down at the car. She really couldn't see much of him, and yet she could feel the dejection he must be feeling, the helplessness. Perhaps he even felt guilt that he was sitting here bored, looking after a woman he considered spoiled and willful, while his friends were out there, doing what he would consider the important jobs. In that car he would have nothing to do except brood about it.

Impulsively, Devon decided what she must do. She threw a housecoat over her pajamas and shoved her feet into a pair of slippers. She went out into the deserted halls, down the elevator and into the dark street.

Grey was out of the car like a shot when she came through the apartment doors.

"What the hell——" His face was like thunder, and his hand on her elbow bit like steel. He spun her around. "March!"

"Grey——" The look on his face should have been enough to make her tremble. She felt perfectly calm.

"Get inside!" He grabbed her keys out of her hand and inserted them in the apartment door, then shoved her through it. He stormed across the lobby with her in tow.

"This is Los Angeles. Where do you think you're going, Devon? The teddy bears' picnic?"

"I wanted to talk to you," she began.

"In your pajamas? You're outside, in the middle of the night, in Los Angeles, in your pajamas, because you had a sudden urge to talk to me? Did you hear a single word I said to you earlier tonight?"

"Don't be stuffy! Nobody saw me."

"What did you want to talk to me about? This better be good, Devon." His voice was grim, his hand still locked on her elbow as the elevator shot upward.

Devon took a deep breath. "I watched the news tonight. I'm so sorry about your colleagues, Grey." Her voice was soft, her eyes locked on his face.

She saw the breath go out of him, and knew she had taken him by surprise. Then the tension left his shoulders and the grim line around his mouth softened.

"You came out in your pajamas to say that?"

"Yes."

He was quiet. The elevator stopped, and they got out. He was still holding her elbow. It felt as if it was on fire, but for some reason she did not try to remove it from his grasp.

"I appreciate your concern," he said. "Now please go back to bed. And please don't run around in your pajamas in public places any more. The natives have been known to riot over less."

She looked down at her ankle-length terry cloth robe. "Hardly," she said wryly.

"Devon, don't pretend to know what men find sexy."

Was he saying that because he found her sexy in her robe, or because he was trying to remove the focus from himself, just the way he did, so skillfully, at school?

"Were they your friends, Grey?" she asked softly.

His answer seemed to catch in his throat. "Yeah," he growled.

She knew better than to try and probe his vulnerability. "Well," she said crisply, "maybe you'd better come in. You'd probably like to be near a phone. And at least if you're in the apartment you could read or watch TV, instead of just sitting there thinking about it."

The hardness had left his eyes. The gray had intensified and she could see the worry and feeling in them. When he spoke his voice was husky with held-in emotion. "Thanks, Devon."

They entered the apartment together. He was looking at her oddly, as if he had never seen her before. As if he had tried not to see her, and now was forced to.

Devon fiddled with the knot on her housecoat. "Help yourself to anything you want," she told him.

"*Merci.*"

"Good night, then."

"Good night, Devon."

She awoke the next morning to the sound of the shower thrumming, and a rich male voice singing.

She stifled a giggle in her pillow. Grey Carmichael had a secret yen for corny country music. He sang it surprisingly well, with an ache and a twang.

She had the coffee ready by the time he emerged from the shower. He was fully dressed, but his hair was towel-roughened and extra dark from being wet.

She smiled at him. "Your friend made it."

He smiled back. "Came off the critical list at around five this morning."

It was the first time she could remember a shared feeling between them. Two human beings experiencing a moment of camaraderie because they had both spent part of the night hoping and praying for the same thing.

"I hope you don't mind about the shower," he added.

"Oh, if terrorists had chosen such an awkward moment to pick on me, I would have thought of something," said Devon.

"Hair spray," he advised solemnly, but his eyes were dancing with wicked humor.

He teased her some more about wearing her housecoat and slippers outside. So she set him to work cooking toast.

He burnt it.

They laughed *together* for the first time.

Devon realized she had never seen him relaxed before, had never seen the wariness washed from his eyes, had never seen him drop his professional watchfulness completely.

When she had told him it would be impossible for him to stay in her apartment, she had thought of how tense it would be, how awkward, what an intolerable invasion of her privacy.

And yet here he was sharing breakfast with her, and it was none of those things.

Grey Carmichael was far more dangerous like this—she knew that. She knew it was more impossible than ever to share her tiny apartment with him. If he was overwhelming when he was curtly and impersonally professional, he was doubly so when he was relaxed, and laughing, and boyishly charming.

So why was she suggesting, her voice tentative, that maybe he could spend his evening shifts in the apartment after all?

The professionalism sprang back in his eyes, the coolness. "Thanks, I'll think about that."

She shrugged with an attempt at indifference. "It's no big deal. I just thought it might be more comfortable for you to sit on the couch than in your car. At least then you could watch the late show."

He was scanning her face, as if searching for some other motivation.

Devon met his questioning gaze coldly. She hoped her eyes were saying, Look, I didn't ask you to go to bed with me, and I don't even want to be your friend. Just for a minute or two, I liked you, and extended a little human kindness to you. If you don't know how to take that, that's your problem.

The stiffness came back between them. It seemed worse than ever. In the staff room at school, Grey picked up a paper and totally shut her out with it.

So when he leaned over, and locked his smoky gray eyes on her with a stunningly smoldering look, she nearly dropped her coffee.

"Thank you for last night," Grey whispered in a stage whisper, and kissed her on the cheek.

She gasped and stared at him, then looked around, flustered. No one seemed to have paid the least bit of attention, thank goodness.

"That wasn't funny, Grey!" she hissed.

He simply grinned devilishly at her.

"Here's those photocopies you wanted."

Devon twisted in her chair to see Alfonso had come in the side door. "Thanks," she stammered. She scanned his face, trying to guess how much he had seen, but his face was expressionless. She took the papers from him and he proceeded to the coffee maker at the other side of the room.

"Isn't he great?" she murmured uncomfortably to Grey, gathering up her things for class. "I just don't know how we'd get by without him."

Grey didn't answer, and she turned and looked at him. He was watching Alfonso, who had slumped in a chair across the room and was reading a comic book. Grey's eyes were narrow, his expression watchful. Then he took half of her load of books from her and sauntered into the hall.

"For heaven's sake," Devon said crossly, once they were safely out of earshot, "don't you think you take suspicion to unreasonable lengths? Alfonso is a wonderful young man. He gives unstintingly of himself to this school, and to my class in particular——"

"Would you ever go out with him?" Grey interrupted her, his question soft, his eyes resting watchfully on her face.

Her jaw dropped and a tiny gasp escaped her. "That's absurd!"

Grey's eyes trailed over her. She had the uneasy idea that he was taking inventory of everything from the small solid gold earrings to her understated silk blouse to her Calvin Klein jeans. And wanted her to know he was taking inventory.

"Absurd," he agreed softly and thoughtfully. "I wonder how Alfonso feels about that particular absurdity?"

"That's ridiculous!" she snapped. "Alfonso doesn't think of me like that."

"Doesn't he? Why not? He's a young man. You're a young woman."

Devon could feel the color drifting up her cheeks. Oh, Lord, what an unmitigated snob she was, and how it hurt to admit it. She had never once considered Alfonso in that light.

"Alfonso would never, ever hurt me," she said defensively. "He didn't write those letters."

Grey said nothing.

"Oh, you're impossibly cynical!"

"Maybe. But it seems to me you should be very careful who you play saint with. I'm sure Joan of Arc was a nice lady too, and look what happened to her."

"I am not playing saint!" she cried. Oh, what a horrible, horrible man! She must have imagined he was good company this morning! She must have been carried away by the momentary insanity caused by a single woman awaking to hear someone singing in her shower! For a while last night and this morning she had thought she had seen beyond his tough mask to a man who was capable of great sensitivity and caring. What a joke! He didn't have feelings! That had just been another of his manipulations. He'd wiggled his way right into her apartment, which was where he had wanted to be all the time. And she'd been blinded enough by him to invite him to stay!

The children began to troop in underneath their flashing eyes.

"Would you mind cleaning out the art supply cupboard while I do reading, Mr. Carmichael?" Devon asked coolly. The cupboard was an absolute mess, the dirtiest job she could think of at such short notice.

But instead of anger, there was faint, mocking amusement in his eyes.

"Your wish is my command," he said blandly.

She realised then that you could dress a prince in rags and make him shovel out the stables, but if he was a real prince, then he would remain one regardless. She had not particularly wanted to know Grey Carmichael was a real prince. No, she had not needed to know that at all.

Once upon a time, Devon had liked this time after school, when a peaceful silence claimed her classroom and she could sit and have a blessed period of uninterrupted time to do some preparation and marking. Now she didn't like it at all. Not with Grey happily hammering away at a broken easel he had found that afternoon.

"Devon." The hammering didn't stop. "Come here!"

She responded to the urgency in his voice. It didn't even occur to her to ask him why.

He set down the hammer as she came across the room. He smiled as she came nearer, reached out his arms and drew her close to him. Of course, she'd been feeling angry with him all day, but now a part of her rose hopefully, thinking, Ah, last night and this morning were real after all.

Still, her brain registered that something was off. But her brain seemed to have shifted into slow gear

as soon as he'd drawn her close to him, and then it
stopped altogether when he murmured, "Kiss me."

For a moment she stared up at him with wide, disbelieving eyes. Again, her brain tried to tell her something, but her eager lips were having no part of it.

Standing on tiptoe, tentatively she brushed her lips
against his.

The arms wrapped more tightly around her, fusing
her soft curves into the hard, uncompromising lines
of his body. His lips accepted the tentative invitation
of hers with breathtaking masculine brutality. His
force pushed her head back and her mouth opened,
and the hot spear of his tongue invaded the cool cavern
of her mouth. The fire spread wildly, until her entire
body was a tortured hotbed of raw feeling.

Somehow she had never quite thought a kiss could
do this. She had occasionally—very occasionally—
experienced the rather mild pleasantness of being
kissed. And occasionally—probably half a dozen
times—she had even been kissed with a wild and wet
passion that had left her repulsed and dismayed.

But this! This searing, drugging, all-consuming fire
that flashed down her limbs, and made her breasts
ache and her head swim, was something she had never,
ever felt before. No, that wasn't true. There had been
a hint of this same sensation when Grey had kissed
her in the lingerie shop. And wasn't this what she had
been yearning for ever since? Without even admitting
it? Yearning for his tongue to twist with hers, and his
teeth to crash against hers, and his strong, iron-hard
hands to press possessively up her sides to the
underside of her breasts, to rest there, tantalizing, a
large thumb working small teasing circles just below
the swell of her breasts.

Her fever seemed to rub out that part of her that had always stood back from her occasional physical contact with the opposite sex, the part that asked, amused and analytical, what the heck am I supposed to do now?

She knew exactly what to do now. She knew exactly when to open her mouth for the rough plundering of his tongue, she knew exactly when to tentatively offer her own tongue in return. His body gave off unmistakable signals of his pleasure when her small hand slipped through the buttons of his shirt to lie tentatively on the hard, heated surface of his stomach. She let her hand trail upward and with awe she felt his nipples harden beneath her touch, and felt the heat from his loins sear through the heavy fabric of her own denims.

His mouth left hers, and her eyes drifted open in bewildered protest. His eyes were open, and not drugged and passionate on her upturned face, but alertly fastened on something over her left shoulder.

In some reserve within her, she found the strength to pull away from him, to back away from the promise of those still hovering lips.

Grey straightened. His eyes trailed to her bruised lips, touched the wild tangle of her hair, and moved over her shoulder again.

"Sorry about that," he said absently. He ran a hand through his own hair.

"I beg your pardon?"

"Someone was looking in the window."

"Oh. You stopped kissing me, because someone was looking in the window?"

"Ah." He looked uncomfortable. "Not exactly."

Understanding hit her like a ton of bricks. "You kissed me because somebody was looking *in* the window?" she asked shrilly. "Answer me, you...you miserable cad!"

"Okay, Devon, I kissed you because somebody was looking in the window."

"You son of a bitch!" But now she knew why her brain had been trying to give her warning signals as she approached him across the room. His tone had not been that of a secret admirer giving in to his long-suppressed libido when he'd asked her to kiss him. No, it had been that of a guerrilla commando. And the smile that had been on his lips had not warmed his eyes. At all. She should have known. She knew she should have known, and she knew *he* knew she should have known. Her anger at herself for having behaved like such a blathering fool increased her anger at him.

"That kid is hungry for something he can't have, Devon—a hunger like that can turn to anger. A very dangerous kind of anger."

"You don't know the first thing about dangerous anger," she said coldly. And then she wound up and hit him as hard as she could across his cheek with her open palm.

The *crack* exploded in the quiet classroom. She actually managed to turn his head. Very slowly he faced her again. His face was absolutely empty of emotion. Devon would have preferred anything to that.

"I'm sorry I hurt you," he said.

A red welt was rising on his face, and she squelched the part of her that wanted to erase it with tender and contrite fingertips.

"My dear Mr. Carmichael, wasn't it you who said you had to care about somebody before they could hurt you?" She turned and stormed away, but her exit gave her far less satisfaction than she needed, because he quietly and calmly followed her out of the room.

Used. He had used the camaraderie that had developed between them last night and this morning. He had taken something genuine and manipulated it to his own ends. He had used it in the coffee room this morning, when Alfonso had appeared. And he had used her again right now.

Devon felt naive, and humiliated. And, despite her denial to him, as hurt as she had ever felt.

It would be a long, cold day in July before she ever gave her tender trust into the keeping of Mr. Grey Carmichael again!

CHAPTER SIX

"DEVON, I think maybe you should go to Redwoods for the weekend."

The car was disgustingly hot. They were stuck in a traffic jam. It was the first either of them had spoken since the sweet promise of that kiss had been so callously betrayed; by his words and motivation; by her angry hand.

She pushed her hair back from her sweaty brow and slanted Grey a glance. He was looking straight ahead, sunglasses hiding his eyes. The angry mark of her hand was still on his cheek, and she cringed from it. She had learned something this afternoon: passion was not something to be trifled with.

"Why don't they put air-conditioning in these cars, for God's sake?" she asked querulously.

She watched a bead of sweat trickle down from his temple, caress the rugged arch of his cheek, and slip down to his chin. She looked away, and felt an urge to open her door, make her way through the maze of hot, growling metal, and walk home along cool, palm tree-shaded pavement.

She toyed with the thought for a moment or two. Grey would be so angry! Why did that seem so appealing? Because at least there were hints of that sizzling passion in his anger, and there were none in the remote stranger who seemed calmly resigned to the traffic?

She glanced again at his profile, and shivered. He looked stern and cool. And she had already learned today that passion was not to be trifled with.

Mercifully, the traffic began to move. The faintest of breezes lifted her heavy hair.

"I want you to go to Redwoods," Grey told her.

"First, it was I *should*, now it's you *want*, and before I know it, I'll just be at Redwoods, won't I?" she burst out angrily. "Why are you pretending I have a choice?"

"Things could heat up, Devon. Now."

So that kiss might make things heat up.

"Lord almighty," she sighed, being deliberately obtuse, "as if it isn't hot enough! How come you don't feel the heat, Grey?" Well, if he could refer to that kiss, so could she. She thumped her forehead. "Oh, how silly of me! Snakes are cold-blooded, aren't they?"

He flinched. After a long time, he spoke, his voice a soft growl. "It was a cold-blooded thing to do. I'm sorry."

"No, you aren't."

The sunglasses were slammed down onto the dashboard. "Damn you, Devon!"

She felt the full force of his grey eyes and refused to cower. She tilted her nose up and looked at him blandly.

"What else can I do, besides apologize?" he asked her testily.

"You aren't sorry. If the very same thing happened again, you'd react the very same way. Your job means more to you than my feelings, and don't try to deny that."

He didn't—though she was rather hoping he would. He slammed his sunglasses back onto his face.

He pulled up in front of her apartment building, and in sizzling silence they went up to her apartment.

He went in first, as was his habit. He did a quick check of the place. He was still wearing his sunglasses even though they were inside.

"Please pack a bag," he ordered quietly.

"I don't want to go to Redwoods."

"You'll be safer there—the house and grounds are far more secure than I can ever make it here. And when you're rattling on about how much my job means to me, you might try to remember you *are* my job right now."

"I knew I didn't have a choice."

"You always have a choice," he said smoothly from behind his sunglasses. "Occasionally I just need to help you make the right one."

"I resent being treated like a child!"

"You resent being treated like a child, and you resent being treated like a woman. Kind of leaves me in a no-win situation, doesn't it?"

"That...that *aberration* that occurred in my classroom was not being treated like a woman. It was being *used*."

"I've had about all I can handle of your trying to lay a guilt trip on me!" Grey snapped angrily. "You enjoyed that kiss, as a woman, and I enjoyed it as a man. If it served another purpose, so what?"

"I knew you weren't sorry!"

"I feel bad that I hurt your feelings. But I kissed you and I enjoyed it. As far as I know that's no longer a hanging offense in this state."

"It's the *so what* I find disturbing."

"Devon, we're a man and a woman thrown together in somewhat stressful conditions. We're living in each other's pockets. Sooner or later, we were going to kiss each other again. Alfonso's playing Peeping Tom just escalated the when."

"I suppose sooner or later you get around to kissing every woman you meet, do you?"

"Woman, I have never met a person who can twist a man's words until they're as mixed up as a braid of bread! Is it so hard for you to accept the fact that I find you attractive?"

Her mouth dropped open. "You do?"

"Oh, for God's sake, Devon!"

"Well, you've certainly never acted like it."

"What do you think that was about in the undies store?"

"You were angry! And it wasn't an *undies* store." She could feel red suffusing her cheeks, which he seemed to find amusing.

"What was it, then?" he challenged.

"It was a lingerie emporium," Devon said snootily.

"I stand corrected. But I don't care how angry I was, I wouldn't have reacted like that if you looked like Mirabelle Webster."

Mirabelle was a teacher on the staff who had an unfortunate liking for chocolate cream puffs—in volume.

"Mirabelle happens to have a beautiful spirit, a fact many superficial people have probably missed," Devon said coldly.

"I haven't. I would willingly accompany Mirabelle to church any time, but I wouldn't kiss her. Ever."

"I suppose I'm supposed to be flattered that you'd kiss me? Is that it?"

"I did my damnedest not to, Devon. I don't mix business and pleasure. But occasionally opportunity knocks so loud and hard——" Grey shrugged. "It happened, and it's over. It won't happen again."

"That's what you said last time."

"Yeah—well, I'm only human. Now, you have ten minutes to pack, or I'll do it for you. And as you've just seen, I'm uneducated in matters you may find important, such as *lingerie* selection."

"You're treating me like a child again!"

"You're acting like one again."

Devon flounced into her bedroom and slammed the door.

"I may act like a child," she called through the door, "but at least I don't use my brute strength to get my way all the time! How bloody mature is that?"

Her door squeaked open and he stood there. The sunglasses were gone. She wished he had left them on; the moody gray of his eyes was riveting.

"Devon, I don't want to trade potshots with you."

"Tough!"

He came across the room. She didn't budge, eyeing him defiantly.

He looked down at her, reached out, and touched her hair—and then her lips.

"It's precisely because you're not a child that I don't want to spend the weekend here with you. Do you understand?"

She stared into his eyes, then nodded. There was safety at Redwoods in more ways than one. It wasn't just the threat to her that was heating up.

It was other things. The heat between two people who have a physical attraction that defied the weak attempts of their intellects to deny it. Who had tasted each other when they shouldn't have tasted. Who had touched each other when they should not have touched. Who had looked into each other's eyes and seen something beyond the roles they were both supposed to play.

He was right—again. It would be safer at Redwoods.

Devon woke up on Saturday morning with a splitting headache. She heard the distinct morning sounds of Redwoods, and scowled. The first thing on her mind on waking had been that kiss, the fact that all her awareness of Grey as a man was up front now instead of below the surface. He knew, and she knew, that it was going to be hard, if not impossible, to go back to the way things had been before.

Grey knew. He knew that something was stirring in her. A virgin at twenty-two, she admitted she was a late bloomer. But she was blooming—an innocent becoming a woman, the sweetness of romantic fantasies giving way to the sharper ache of reality. Of yearning to know the secrets of herself she had never known; the secrets of her body, the depth and breadth of her passion, the way her softness was made to cleave to a man's hardness.

What a terrible time for a man like Grey to show up in her life! A man who did everything with a subtle aura of innate sensuality, a man so incredibly comfortable with his masculinity.

Well, her alarm had gone off the minute she had seen him. She just hadn't known that it was the alarm on her biological clock.

She vowed she would never again let him get so much as a glimpse of this dawning side of her, that he was both wittingly and unwittingly coaxing to the surface. It was bad enough that he had so totally invaded her physical world. She wasn't giving him one inch of her emotional one!

She got out of bed, a rueful captive of this force that lived and breathed and danced its own life within her. Her passion, her desire.

It simply wasn't listening to her stern reminders that Grey was definitely not the man to fall in love with.

Not that she was that naive. Love didn't have a thing to do with what she felt for him. Her body was straining to answer one of Mother Nature's timed commands. It was about as romantic as eating when you were hungry, if you stopped to think about it.

She came down the stairs, her most carefree smile pasted on her face.

"Good morning," she greeted Mike Wilson, and the man who stood cheerfully beside him.

"This is Grey's replacement . . ."

Her smile froze to her lips. His replacement?

" . . . Dan Nelligan."

It seemed she was looking at the replacement from a long distance away. She noted, abstractedly, and with a distinct uncaring, that he was probably one of the most handsome men she had ever seen. He was extremely tall, broad-shouldered, blond-haired, with dancing brown eyes.

"How do you do?" she said frostily, the layer of ice, that never fooled Grey, effectively keeping her turmoil from these eyes trained to probe.

Where was Grey? When would she ever see him again? Had he gone because he knew her feelings were heating up inside her? Becoming harder to control? Would he be in danger? Would people be shooting at him? At Grey? Thank goodness, she had known all along—had known better than to invest even a simple liking into a man that people shot at.

"Are you all right?" asked Mike anxiously.

"Fine," she chirped cheerfully. "Low blood sugar. I'd better have breakfast." She wondered if that even made sense.

Everything she said seemed to make absolute sense to Mike Wilson. He was grinning as if she'd been adorably witty.

"Next time Grey has days off, I'll make sure *I'm* assigned to you," he declared.

Devon watched him walk away, and vaguely registered his adoration. But another part of her was registering the words days off. Days off? Days off!

Her heart began to beat again. She could feel warm blood began to pulse through her deadened limbs. "When will Grey—Mr. Carmichael—be back?" Could that casual, remote voice belong to her?

"Monday morning," Dan told her. He lowered his voice. "He said to tell you he'd be there in time for school."

He'd left a message and that was it? Devon didn't know whether to be annoyed that he'd seen fit to share her secret with yet another stranger, or grateful that he'd known it would be important to her that he would be back in her classroom on Monday morning. That she wouldn't want to have yet another person disrupting her schedule, her pupils, her professional life.

"Grey didn't mention that he was going to have days off," she said. She tried to sound casual, but instead she sounded stiff.

Had he known, yesterday, that he would not be here for the weekend? She suspected he had known no such thing. But she wouldn't have put it past him that, given the growing physical tension between them, Grey had pulled out all the stops to get away from her. Which she should be very grateful for!

"We're incredibly short of manpower right now," Dan told her. "Time off is at a premium, but I guess Grey had priority. He probably won't get any more for a while, so I wouldn't count on the kid being assigned to you the next time."

"The kid?" she queried.

"Wilson."

"Oh." There was no charitable way to say she couldn't care a less if Mike Wilson jumped in the lake.

"He's a bit green," Dan explained. "Grey requested someone with a little more seniority."

"Isn't my father's life being entrusted to the 'kid'?" she asked dryly, though a small part of her registered that comment and turned it into *he cares about me*.

Careful! she warned herself. That dawning sense of libido was probably capable of making mountains out of molehills in order to have its wicked way.

"It seems unlikely your father would slide off his balcony," Dan said with dry humor.

"He told you that?" she demanded. She went from feeling cautiously cared about to feeling horrendously betrayed. Had Grey and the guys sat around having a good laugh at her expense?

Grey wasn't even here, and her emotions were still yo-yoing up and down at the end of his strings! That insensitive cad! How dared he reveal something like that about her—something that showed her in such a poor light?

"He told me everything I needed to know to do my job," Dan assured her. "I guess we both think keeping you safe is a pretty important job."

This was said with such polished sincerity that she couldn't help but smile. Dan Nelligan was lethally charming, and she suspected from his easy return of her smile that he knew it. Still, she suspected he was going to be good fun to be around. And there were too many undertows between her and Grey for it ever to be fun. Even when they managed a cease-fire, during her working hours, that undercurrent, that sizzling undercurrent of awareness, kept it from being enjoyable.

"Maybe we could go riding after breakfast," Dan suggested. Devon shot him a surprised look.

"That's why I'm *really* here," he teased. "I'm top-notch at my job, *and* I know how to ride."

It was silly to feel a glow of pleasure, to feel, once again, cared about. It was only logical that Grey would request someone who knew how to ride. None the less, it made her feel cared about all over again.

Dan Nelligan knew how to ride. And how to tell a story. And how to make her laugh. They got along wonderfully, and it was a refreshing relief to be with a man who was so easy to be with. And yet she had a strange sense of *missing*. She couldn't even say what. She supposed that when a wind blew, whistling and lonely, even though it made you uncomfortable, when it stopped you missed it, in some strange way cocked your head waiting for its return, and the majesty and untameable spirit that were as much a part of it as the discomfort had been.

Early on Monday morning, Dan drove her into Los Angeles. He had her weak with laughter by the time they pulled into the school parking lot.

She saw Grey standing inside the shadow of the door, his face sombre, waiting for her.

She turned and smiled at Dan, her smile genuine enough, but a shade or two brighter for the benefit of the man watching. "I had a lovely time this weekend. You're a fun person to be around," she told him.

Dan's own easygoing smile was gone, for once. "I really enjoyed it too. Devon, do you suppose I could see you again some time? Maybe for dinner or..."

When his voice trailed away, she looked back at him, realizing too late that as soon as he had started to speak, her eyes had moved to Grey.

"Oh." Dan's easygoing smile was back in place. "That's the lie of the land, is it?"

"What?" she protested.

He too looked at Grey. "I know I seem pretty casual, but I don't miss much." He nodded toward Grey. "He's a good man, one of the best. But his job is his jail. It's made him hard. And it's made him lonely."

"And it didn't do that to you?" Devon pretended a total lack of interest in Grey.

He sighed. "Different men react to stress in different ways. I'm a better actor than Grey—I don't know if that's to my credit or not."

Devon thought of the "fun" they'd had this weekend—underneath it, he'd been every bit as wary and watchful as Grey. And suddenly she didn't know whether it was to his credit or not either. Somewhere along the line she'd developed an appreciation for honesty, for the gut-level communication—the realness—she could expect from Grey.

Unexpectedly, Dan leaned over and caught her unsuspecting lips in his.

"Couldn't resist." He grinned at her stunned expression. "That's another difference between Grey and me. Sometimes I break the rules. He never does."

"Rules?"

"Personal involvement on the job. It's a no-no. Good thing Grey isn't a tattletale, or I'd probably wind up a store detective at Harry's Five and Dime!" His expression became solemn again. "Consider it a goodbye present from me. When Grey kissed you in the classroom, he was flushing out a suspect—seeing if he could provoke an unguarded reaction, accelerate the situation with Alfonso into reaching its natural conclusion. I just did the same thing."

"You knew he kissed me?" she stammered. How could he do that to her? How could he make such a fool of her, and then tell somebody else about it?

Dan eyed her sympathetically, then sighed. "Yeah, I knew. It was in his report."

In his report, Devon echoed mentally and numbly. She wondered what he'd written, how he'd managed to describe that blisteringly passionate kiss in coldly dispassionate terms.

Somehow, she did not know how, she managed to get out of the car without crying. She managed to walk past Grey and into that school with her head high and her manner cool, as if she hadn't just suffered the grossest humiliation of her entire life.

Grey fell into step beside her, his eyes probing. She ducked her head so that the silky curtain of her hair kept his shrewd gaze out until she had time to compose herself.

"Have a nice weekend?" he asked smoothly.

Devon hazarded a glance at his profile. That telltale little muscle in his jaw was working wildly. He was angry—very angry.

"I had a fabulous weekend," she told him shortly.

"It certainly looks like it," he rejoined crisply. "You look as if you've been sucking lemons."

"Thank you. You're not exactly a candidate for Miss America yourself."

"I agree. My measurements probably put me out of the running. Not that I was too broken up. My childhood dream was to be a firefighter."

"Firefighters and Miss America have more in common than you might think. I believe integrity is a necessary component in either of those jobs. You're much better suited for slinking around."

"I don't happen to agree that I slink around. I do a tough job, and I do it with pride—and integrity, as a matter of fact."

"Really? How did you describe our little liaison of last Friday in your report? Did you say, with great integrity, of course, that you kissed me with convincing passion for poor Alfonso? Did you say I kissed you back? Did you say I pressed myself into you like a wanton——?"

"Devon, don't."

His voice sounded pained. Wasn't it too bad that he should be on the receiving end of pain instead of the dishing-out end?

"Don't?" she echoed. "Mr. Carmichael, I haven't even begun. I may write a report, and sell it to one of those magazines with the cheap pages that leave black ink all over your hands. That blare headlines like 'He seduced her to get his man.'"

"Be quiet!" he snapped. "The walls have ears."

Devon stopped and stared at him defiantly. "So I spent the whole weekend at Redwoods and nothing heated up, after all, Grey? Your suspect didn't bomb a few buildings because he was so upset to see me kissed?"

"I just told you to watch it."

"Watch it yourself," she snapped back. "Skinny little Alfonso is a ridiculous suspect."

She moved by him again, walked into the brightness of her empty classroom.

"Dan Nelligan was a wonderful change from you," she commented tightly. "We had a very pleasant weekend. I don't find him at all bossy or argumentative. I don't suppose there's any chance of a permanent switch, is there?"

Grey's face was a mask of indifference, but she noticed with great satisfaction that that informative little muscle in his jaw that jerked when he was angry was working spasmodically at the moment.

"There's no chance of that," he said firmly. "None."

"Too bad!"

"Good old Dan," he bit back. "The future father of our nation."

Devon turned from straightening her desk and gave him a surprised look. "Dan is ambitious politically?"

"Dan is ambitious about one thing and one thing only, and it's got nothing to do with politics."

She gasped, and was immediately sorry, since Grey seemed immensely satisfied with her shocked reaction. Flushed again, like a bird before bush beaters, she thought wearily.

"That's not a very nice thing to say about your friend," she observed.

He shrugged a big shoulder. "He'd be the first to admit it."

She knew he was right. That was what Dan had been trying to tell her, she supposed. Different men handled the stress of a difficult job in different ways—Grey by isolating himself, and Dan by becoming a ladies' man, losing himself in a thousand superficial relationships. Somehow, once she thought about it, her instinct had told her that about Dan far before Grey's revelations. Which didn't mean she couldn't like him.

She pretended to be busy at her desk.

"Have you seen Alfonso, FBI's-most-wanted, yet?" she asked. "I need some papers run off."

"Alfonso hasn't come in yet. My money says he won't."

A shiver of misgiving traveled up her spine. Alfonso had never missed school. Suddenly it didn't seem quite so irrational to see him as a suspect. And suddenly she was glad of Grey's physical presence in her room. His mastery in his chosen field was simply beyond reproach. Too bad his human skills had suffered because of his dedication to excellence in his work.

She hazarded another glance at him. He'd moved to the window and was looking out—casually, an uninformed observer might have thought. But she knew it wasn't casual. She could tell by the way he didn't quite turn his back to the door, by the way his pewter-colored eyes continually roved the hard concrete playground.

He must have sensed her eyes on him, because he turned his head suddenly and their eyes locked head-on.

"Why did you feel compelled to put it in your report that you kissed me?"

"Another thing about Dan is that he talks too much," Grey said flatly.

"Well, that's a darned sight better than not talking enough! Most women are sick to death of the strong, silent type—who, incidentally, are not supposed to kiss and tell!"

"I said in my report that I had every reason to believe Alfonso Smithers to be our number one suspect. I said I felt that he had deep and twisted feelings for you. I said that it was my opinion that he could continue penning poison letters for years, unless something happened to force his hand. I said I made a professional decision to kiss you in the event that Alfonso's jealousy would bring on the next stage in his tangled game."

"Alfonso is not the leader of any terrorist group!" Devon snapped. *A professional decision.*

"Correct."

"Then why is he your suspect?"

"I don't think there are any terrorists. I think one rather pathetic young man, with a malicious warp to his mind, is probably the Heart of the Ghetto. It was his unfortunate luck to be a poor speller who stumbled on the code name Hart, which is the top secret Government project your father is producing at his factory, and arousing all kinds of suspicion. His bad luck may have been your good luck. Without the link to the Government contract, you would never have received this kind of attention."

"I'm afraid I haven't yet developed the perspective to see one single thing since the day you walked into my life qualifying for the term 'good luck.'"

"I think he's dangerous, Devon. And that's why I feel compelled to flush him out. The Government won't foot the bill for your protection forever—particularly if there isn't the threat to their contract that they assumed."

"That's very cold-blooded."

"Yeah. And that's why I'm working fast. And maybe that's why I seem cold-blooded sometimes too."

"For my protection," she snorted.

"In more ways than one," Grey muttered, his gaze suddenly on her lips, intense and brooding.

He thought she needed protection from him! As if she were Red Riding Hood and he was the Big Bad Wolf.

"How very thoughtful of you," she stated coldly.

"Maybe. Maybe I'm looking out for my own back."

"In what way?"

"They say hell hath no fury..."

She stared at him, absolutely and utterly aghast. How could this man do this to her over and over? String her along just to cut her loose; lift her up high just to dash her down.

"I wouldn't give you the opportunity of scorning me if you were the last ape on this planet, Mr. Carmichael!" she snapped.

He looked satisfied—and sad too.

By insinuating that she might report that kiss to his superiors if he turned down any other advances from her, he'd pushed her away as successfully as if he'd done it with all his superior brute strength.

Imagine her debating—even in a moment of near insanity—whether this might be the man she would lose her virginity to. Why, she hated him!

But suddenly, looking at the rigid, proud way he held his shoulders, and at the carefully schooled invulnerability of his face, she could hear Dan saying, "The job is his jail. It's made him hard. And it's made him lonely."

She had a sudden bizarre impulse to reach out her hand and tell him she knew the way home. Except she didn't. Perhaps her heart did, but what kind of a fool trusted something like a heart?

It had proved its treacherousness already, silly old heart. Couldn't it listen to her head? Her head telling her, in no uncertain terms, not to get involved with this man. Because if she got involved with him, despite her best intentions she would love him. And if she loved him, some day she might marry him. And if you married a man like Grey Carmichael the chances of being a very young widow seemed undesirably high.

She'd been the one who had told him that to the right woman his job wouldn't matter. Obviously she was not the right kind of woman. Which she knew!

The voice of her desire, of her passion, had to get in one parting shot, however. It asked her if it might not be infinitely better to be a young widow who had loved than a bitter old maid who had not.

CHAPTER SEVEN

SCHOOL was out for the day. Her students had gone home. The day had felt endless, and now Devon forced herself to do small tasks to get ready for tomorrow. Her head ached, a victim of her very mixed-up emotions toward that large, brooding figure at the back of her classroom.

She simply could not sort out how she really felt about Grey. She resented him and disliked him. He had intruded in her life and he was overbearing and unapologetic about it. She felt suffocated by his nearness.

And yet...and yet he stirred her blood. In unexpected moments, when the shield came down from his gray eyes, she felt a perturbing sense of tenderness for him.

She sighed. Once, when she was young, her father had taken her to Banff, in the heart of the Canadian Rockies. The mountains had affected her like this too. At first they had made her feel suffocated, and small and closed in. And then, slowly and subtly, before she had even realized what was happening, she had begun to appreciate them, to see the rugged beauty, to feel set free by them instead of hemmed in.

She supposed that just went to show that if you were exposed to anything for long enough you would start to have reluctant feelings for it.

As a child, she had felt she loved those mountains too. They had spent three weeks there, hiking and horseback riding, going up gondolas, swimming in natural sulphur hot springs. She had felt so sad when they had had to go, and vowed she would go back there, year after year after year. She had even made a wild pledge that she would return some day, as a forest ranger or a parks worker. But she had got home, and her childish oaths, and even those beloved mountains, had been forgotten with amazing quickness. Her relationship with Grey would be just like that. Hah! It was stretching it to call it a relationship. The impact of his powerful presence would start to dissipate as soon as he was gone. He would be a memory, like those mountains, only faintly disturbing, instead of pleasant.

But you have more maturity than that twelve-year-old child, the voice of her desire chided her.

Hah! she snapped back. That's exactly why I know better than to play with fire. To even *contemplate* fire.

She sighed and placed what her students called a "stinky" sticker on the last worksheet she had marked. They loved the stickers, that smelled vaguely of grapes and bubble-gum and chocolate. The day had finished with circle time, and the desks were still in a circle. Devon went over with the marked work sheets, leaving them on the appropriate desks, managing to smile as she pictured Francie's squeal of delight, Ralph's slow, shy, disbelieving smile that she'd given him a sticker despite the fact that he'd only struggled through two questions, and got both of them wrong...

A strangled sound and a flash of movement startled her out of her reverie, and she turned questioning eyes toward Grey.

He was charging toward her, and for a stunned moment she watched him with a detached sort of appreciation. His motion seemed oddly slowed, each movement delineated. She could see every muscle in his legs strain as he surged across the room, could feel the rigid tension in the pumping of his arms. His hair was flying back, as though he were running full out in an open meadow, and his face was...

His face was grim and determined, an expression like pain etched into his features. When he looked like that, how could she still marvel at how he had gone from stillness to full out in a split second, like a lion shifting from its almost languid stalking posture to the full awesome power of its pursuit?

It registered, somewhere in that split second, that he was going to hit her at that tremendous speed, and her mouth formed into a surprised O that never sounded.

He crashed through the desks that surrounded her, scattering them like leaves before the wind. With surprising hardness and hurt his arms wrapped around her waist, and she could feel his thigh muscles coiling, then she was lifted off the ground, propelled through the air for a heart-stopping moment, then being ground into the floor, his tremendous weight and force pushing the air from her. There was an explosion of sound, the scattering tinkle of shattering glass, at the same time as they hit the floor.

Devon couldn't breathe. He was right on top of her, crushing the life out of her. Pure animal panic rose in her, then was quieted, strangely enough, by his scent filling her nostrils, spicy and soapy and masculine.

Her brain seemed to still be in slow motion, operating as it had when she had watched him running. Grey on top of her, hard and hurting, covering her

whole body...his hand pushing her face ruthlessly
into the rock wall of his chest...shattering glass...

"Somebody shot at us," she said, her voice calm,
disembodied, curious, but unalarmed.

The weight lifted of her suddenly. Grey squatted
beside her. The comforting scent ebbed. Her shoulders
began to shake and her jaw quivered.

"Devon, it wasn't a shot. Calm down." He got up,
his eyes flicking around the room, searching for
something. She was stunned by his abruptness. She
felt as if she was in shock, but obviously she had better
not expect any sympathy from him!

"Calm down?" She didn't like the way he said that,
as if she were an overly emotional woman who had
just caught a glimpse of Paul Newman. She sat up,
and dragged a hand through the tangle of her hair,
determined not to let him see how close to panic she
had come, though the feeling seemed to be receding
now. "How do you know it wasn't a shot? It sounded
like a shot to me."

He was investigating the broken glass at the window,
looking out at the schoolyard with searching eyes.
"Damn," he muttered to himself. He sent her a dis-
paraging glance. "When was the last time you heard
a shot?"

Devon thought about that, her mind still working
slowly for some reason. Had she ever heard a real
shot? Or just on movies? Of course, now and then
she had thought a backfiring car...

Grey's eyes caught on something and he moved
swiftly across the room. "Here it is."

"What?" She scrambled to her feet.

"It's just a baseball."

"It is not." He had never lied to her before. No wonder! It was very evident when he was lying.

He was trying to put the object in his pocket.

"What is it?" she demanded, grabbing his hand and trying to pry it open.

"Devon, cut it out!"

"I want to see!"

"It's only a rock. Haven't you ever seen a rock before?"

Devon pried open his hand marginally. She could see the crumpled paper attached to the rock with elastic bands. She let go of his hand, realizing that force was not the method to use on Grey.

"That note belongs to me," she said calmly.

"Fat chance!"

"It's probably protected by U.S. Postage laws."

"Nice try."

"Give it to me," she ordered sweetly, "or I'll scream rape at the top of my voice."

Grey handed her the rock as if it was heated. "I'm surprised you haven't tried that particular threat before, Devon."

"Me too," she agreed, scanning his face suspiciously. Something was not ringing true. Grey simply was not bested this easily. "What are you up to, Carmichael?"

"Up to?" he asked innocently.

She glared at him, now certain that he was looking at her with amusement ... and satisfaction.

"You just stopped me from panicking, didn't you?" she deduced.

"I'm not good with hysterical women."

"I would not have become hysterical!"

"Oh, sure. A gunshot, for pity's sake! You watch too many movies."

"Oh, and you came hurtling across the room like a linebacker for the San Francisco Giants because you thought it was a rock?"

"Did I hurt you?" he evaded. "I hit you pretty hard."

"Yes, you did—hard and below the belt. I've never done one single thing to suggest to you that I might be the hysterical type."

"You were going to start crying."

"I most certainly was not. And crying is a far cry from *hysteria*."

"Devon, I just made a snap judgment. I didn't think it would be wise to take you in my arms and comfort you, no matter how badly you wanted me to."

"I wanted you to? You egotistical boor! Nothing was further from my mind!" Devon blushed red. She *had* momentarily craved the comfort of his strong, protective arms.

His expression told her she was no better at lying than he was.

"All right," she conceded angrily, "maybe I did want a bit of comfort. Would that have been so awful for you? Would giving someone who'd been frightened a minute's comfort just have been too much of a chore for you? Or would it just be too much of a letdown from the normal drama of your life? I mean, a human being feeling fear just can't compete, can it? Not with blazing pistols. Beautiful Russian spies——"

"I'm sorry I ever shared that particular daydream with you."

She ignored him. "Incognito meetings with Mafia dons. Camping trips in the Colombian jungle——"

"You're very upset," he pointed out, his tone mildly condescending in her ears.

"I am? I don't know why I should be. Heavens, I get shot at routinely."

"It wasn't a shot."

"Oh, quit splitting hairs! Are you so insensitive and callous that you can't even console another human being?"

"Devon, I get into trouble every time I touch you. I decided to leave it alone this time. You should be glad."

"Come to think of it, I am. As if I'd want your big hairy paws all over me!"

"Now, that's the Devon I know," he grinned. "Welcome back. Could we get on to business? The note?"

Devon gave him one final icy look, pried the note from the rock, and smoothed it with her hand.

The writing was an angry scratch, done in red ink that had dribbled in places, giving it a look of violence to match the tone of the words:

> yu haf hurt my hart
> kising him was not very smart
> he is a cop
> and next time it wont be a rok

"Oh, God!" She brought her fist up to her mouth and bit down hard on it, but it wasn't enough. The tears sprang to her eyes and rolled down her cheeks. Coupled with the rock, it was too shocking an intrusion into her life.

Grey gently took the note from her. She turned her back on him and wept.

"Devon," he said softly.

"Leave me alone!"

"Devon..."

"I'm...not...hysterical. I'm just sad."

"I know that." He came around, and his arms enfolded her. A strong hand came up and pushed her head gently into the hard wall of his chest. "There isn't a man alive who can resist a crying woman," he said softly, as if he needed to rationalize it.

"Oh, get your hairy paws off me!" It came out an unconvincing whisper. Instead of letting go, the comforting bands of his arms tightened around her.

The sobs took her again, more quietly this time. Surrounded by his warmth and his scent, she felt safe and warm, like a small child being comforted after a bad dream. She cried and cried. Grey stroked her hair, awkwardly at first, like a big man patting a small dog. But somewhere his touch changed. She could tell he had begun to feel the texture of her hair, and was enjoying the sensation of it running, like liquid silk, through his callused hands.

His fingertips moved, soothingly, slowly tracing the path of her tears down her cheeks to her neck. He lightly massaged the tension from the top of her spine.

Her tears were drying up. She hiccuped, and he tugged playfully on one of her ears. She pulled her nose out of his chest and looked up at him blearily.

"I'm sorry, I——"

"Your mascara's running." His eyes were fixed on hers as though that ridiculous fact fascinated him, made him extraordinarily aware of her as a woman. Aware of her softness and vulnerability.

She took a swipe at her eyes, but he stayed her hand. He placed one of each of his sun-browned hands on either side of her pale face and forced her to return his steady, searching gaze. She forgot her mascara.

Then his mouth, exquisitely seeking, dropped down over hers, and the last of her anguish was chased away by the moist heat of his lips.

She melted into his strength, into the hard heat of his body. The utterly masculine scent of his sweat stirred some deep primal urge within her. His manner was gentle, at first, questioning, until exactly the moment he felt her own lips whisper an answer against his. Then his questing kiss became more demanding, recognized her strength, and asked her to give in return.

And she did, running the tip of her tongue over the sharp edges of his teeth, nudging the rough surface of his tongue with hers.

A shiver of white-hot heat raced through her. And then another, and another, until she was vibrating like a wild thing caught in a cage. Her nerve endings were tingling with alertness and a gnawing anticipation.

He read her signals, her supple body giving out unmistakable signs of delight, of wanting, of needing. His hands began a bold exploration, tracing delicate patterns over her shoulder, her hip, her spine, her buttock. He left a trail of fire in his wake. He released two of the buttons on the front of her blouse, and that ardent hand burned a tantalizing track over her stomach, then dipped down below the waist of her jeans.

Fire—oh, precious fire! She had never burned with this kind of heat, never been warmed by this fierce kind of radiance. She had never before been drawn into the heart of the flame, become so absorbed in a single moment that she felt as though she'd been inhaled into the sweltering core of a blast furnace. She was exquisitely uncomfortable, tortured, anguished. She was beside herself with yearning for something she did not know, had never known, and yet *knew* she was ready for. Something that would wash over her like cool water, gently extinguishing the inferno, until a certain man, with a certain touch, certain eyes, certain hands, stoked the blaze to near flash point again.

Something hit the window, and a squeal of fright escaped her. She tried to jerk away from him, but he held her close.

"It was only a ball," he assured her. "Can't you hear the kids playing basketball out there?"

She could now. How was it that she could be lost in a very private world, and he had probably known the exact moment the children arrived with their basketball? She supposed it was his job, and that he was very good at it, but it wasn't very flattering to her.

A shiver racked her, and the heat ebbed from her passion, doused with icy fingers.

"What is it?" he asked softly.

"I feel . . . as if I'm being watched, now. As if he'll come back. As if I'd better never let my guard down. As if kissing you is inviting his rage." She hesitated. "As if maybe you're only kissing me to invite his rage. I don't want to be the star of your five o'clock report again."

Grey released her abruptly. A pain burned through his eyes, but then it was masked.

Her anxiety shimmered heavy in the air, choking, like debris after an explosion, before it settled, and became dust beneath their feet. She found no comfort in Grey's cold eyes.

"He's going to come after me, isn't he?" she said quietly.

"Yes." His tone became grim. So did his face.

A part of her mourned the tenderness she had chased away.

She made herself ask the question she dreaded. "Who was it? Did you see?"

"I saw him. That's why I was running toward you before the rock even came through the window. I could tell by the expression on his face——"

She took a deep breath. "Who was it?"

"You know who it was, Devon."

"Yes." She did know. She had been examining her feelings for Alfonso ever since Grey had announced that he was the number one suspect. In a very short time she had gone from utter disbelief to uneasy acceptance.

"When I first met him, he made me very nervous," she admitted slowly. "And my jittery feelings had made me feel guilty. It seemed that he was trying so hard to overcome his bad breaks. He gave so much to the school and the children. It seemed awful not to like him. I felt that I was shallow and superficial, because when I was presented with a real live disadvantaged person I felt anxious and troubled instead of caring and altruistic.

"So I tried to like him. I forced myself to overcome what I felt was my pettiness and my inbred prejudice. I actually fooled myself into accepting him, when I should have been listening to my intuition, the voice that would have kept me safe."

Grey nodded, his eyes less cold, wry understanding in them, as if he had seen that all the time. "Always trust that first instinct, that gut feeling. That very first thing you *feel* before your brain gets in there and corrupts your instinct with all the rules of polite society that your intellect holds so dearly to. That particular realization has saved my skin more than once."

He regarded her thoughtfully, then shoved his hands deep into his jeans pockets. "Dammit, Devon, you look so sad."

"I am." The tears threatened again, but she prevented them from spilling. "I thought he was my friend. I thought he liked me."

"I think he did, Devon. But his trust in mankind had been mutilated long before you entered the picture. I could see that in his eyes, in the way he carried himself. It probably wasn't very long before his liking started to twist itself into a bizarre kind of hunger, and then into anger at you for wielding power over his heart."

Now she really did feel sad for Alfonso. "What will happen to him?" she asked.

"I don't know. It depends how much more aggressive he manages to get before we catch him. At the moment, he's in fairly serious trouble."

"He needs psychiatric help, Grey."

"I'm not a judge."

"But couldn't you——"

"Devon, most criminal types are not exactly healthy, socially well-adjusted people. I just do my——" He stopped, staring into the bleakness of her eyes. "Okay," he sighed, "I'll do what I can for him."

"Thank you." She paused, another thought dawning on her. "He'd know where I live, wouldn't he?"

"The letters were all delivered to Redwoods, but I think he knows where you live. He probably followed you there more than once. You'd probably be shocked by what he knows about you."

Devon felt violated, her world, her sense of safety and security, raped by an exploding window in the middle of a sunny California afternoon.

"I don't want to go back there, to the apartment. And not to Redwoods either."

"Okay."

She hugged herself, and asked in a small voice, "But where can I go where I'll feel safe?" She wondered if she would ever feel completely safe again.

"You can come home with me."

She started, then stared at him. She could tell he already regretted the impulse that had made him say that.

Still, she felt completely safe again.

Though considering what had just transpired between them it was possible she was buying one kind of safety at the price of another.

"Nothing will happen," Grey said harshly.

"I didn't say it would!"

"I'm far too old for you."

"You're not kidding!"

"And too experienced."

"Oh, la-de-da!"

"I know you probably think I cut a fairly romantic figure—— "

"I think no such thing!"

"—but you can forget any plans you have for seducing me. I'm not interested in vulnerable young women. I'm particularly not interested in a virgin," Grey finished.

"You seem to be conveniently forgetting who's been assaulting who!" she told him angrily. "And as for my being a virgin, that's an interesting titbit. Is that written in my file?"

"It's written all over you."

She closed her eyes in exasperation. "Grey, I'm tired and I'm hungry. I want to eat Italian food until I nearly explode, and then I want to crawl into a warm, soft, safe bed—alone. Is that abundantly clear to you? Do you hear me, or has your hot-air-balloon-size ego put you in orbit yet?"

"I hear you," he said mildly, "and I know where to find the world's greatest Italian food."

"Oh, wow," she said dryly. "He has a redeeming quality."

Devon felt exhausted, both from the events of the afternoon and from fencing with Grey. She noticed he was giving the heavy afternoon traffic his full attention, as if he were a businessman driving home from a normal day at the office. He looked as fresh and unperturbed as he had when they had started out this morning.

Of course, for him, this probably *was* a normal day at the office!

He stopped at a small Italian café that he said wasn't far from his place. "It doesn't look like much, but the food is superb," he assured her.

He was greeted in robust Italian by a man wearing a checkered apron. He responded in kind and they were escorted, by the beaming proprietor, to a cozy high-walled wooden booth at the back. Devon wondered if he always sat facing the door like an old-fashioned gunslinger.

"I didn't know Italian was one of your languages," she remarked.

"It isn't. I just have a smattering—mostly from eating here. I pick up languages really easily. Of course, I grew up fluent in two, which seems to make it easier to pick up new languages. My mother was French."

He chatted on about himself, and it was such a novelty, and Devon was so reluctantly intrigued by him, that she didn't realize until later that he was deliberately relaxing her, putting her at ease, trying to untie the rather large knot of tension that sat like a rock in the bottom of her belly.

Even when she'd caught on to it, she didn't care. She wanted to hear about him, his background, his adventures.

She put away most of the steaming dish of ravioli that had been set in front of her. The food was tangy and delicious. So was the red wine that Grey kept refilling her glass with.

At some point, she noticed he was not partaking of the wine himself.

"Don't you think you might find a drink relaxing after our adventure this afternoon?" she asked.

"I very rarely drink. Especially *not* after something like that," he said easily.

His job was back, in the center of the table, right between them.

"Might let your guard down?" she guessed. "Or say something better left unsaid?"

"I just don't believe in distorting reality."

"Humph! You certainly have been plying me with the stuff. No problems with distorting my reality?"

"I also don't believe in taking advantage of a lady who's been imbibing a little too much," Grey added.

She eyed him narrowly. "I told you I wasn't interested."

He laughed. "It's human nature to be interested, Devon. I think that stuff," he nodded at the glass of wine, "was invented just so that nature could have a chance to get past the fortifications of our reserve. That's part of the reason it wouldn't be a good idea for both of us to get into it."

Devon looked at the wine in her long-stemmed glass in a faintly new light. Come to think of it, she wanted every ounce of her reserve to be solidly in place tonight. Discreetly, she pushed the wine to one side.

Of course, it might be too late, she acknowledged. She did feel wonderfully languid and relaxed.

"So how do you recover from the shock of being assaulted by flying rocks or bullets or whatever else you get thrown at you in the line of duty?" she queried.

He laughed softly. "My fear of horses keeps getting worse."

"Are you saying you aren't afraid? Weren't?"

"Of course I was afraid. And I'm not going to say you ever get used to being afraid. But I've got pretty good at returning to normal quickly once the danger has passed. I'd be a basket case if I didn't."

Meaning he's in danger all the time, she thought wearily.

"It would be very silly to fall for a man like you," she muttered, her tongue somewhat loosened by her third glass of wine.

"Very," he agreed.

"So what if somebody did? Fall for you?"

He was silent for a long time, eyeing the refraction in his water glass. The he looked up, unsmiling.

"I already told you I'm not a very romantic figure. But I guess if somebody were foolish enough to 'fall for me,' as you put it..." He paused thoughtfully. "I guess falling for anybody means learning to accept them exactly as they are. And learning to accept that life makes no promises. A businessman could get hit by a bus crossing the street. My best friend during high school died at twenty-seven of cancer. He was a gardener. You can't get into a much less hazardous career than that."

"But if you loved a person very much, couldn't you ask them to quit courting danger?"

"No."

"Oh."

"I don't think love is about controlling, Devon," said Grey. "I don't think it's about pretty pictures, and slippers in front of the fire. I don't even think love is always the most pleasant of emotions."

He had her there. He was right; it wasn't about pretty pictures, or slippers. It was about this desire that burned in her belly, and this ache that burned in her soul. No, love did not seem to be about controlling. If it was, she'd simply choose to fall in love with someone dull and predictable like Mr. Peters, the principal of her school.

And she had not fallen in love with Mr. Peters.

Or Grey either, she reminded herself sharply.

But, looking into the candlelight-darkened depths of his gray eyes, she felt fear that put the fear of her glass-shattered afternoon to shame.

CHAPTER EIGHT

GREY'S apartment was on the top floor of an old turn-of-the-century renovated house.

They climbed the outside stairs, then he reached past Devon and inserted a key into a door with a leaded glass window and jerked it open. He flipped on a light.

The room was illuminated in gentle gold. And it was, for some unfathomable reason, the most welcoming room she had ever been in. One large room had been artfully turned into a living room, kitchen, dining area and study. The odd angles and slopes of the ceiling had been used to separate areas—it was low over the kitchen, high over the living room, sloping over the desk set in a floor-to-ceiling window alcove. The floors were polished hardwood, with rugs scattered over them. There were skylights in each section of the apartment.

His taste was eclectic. He'd set off his living room with an invitingly plump sectional sofa, several casual chairs and several coffee tables. The dining-room set was turn-of-the-century, pioneer art in pine, a match for the desk in the alcove. The kitchen was gleaming twentieth-century efficiency. And everywhere there was a spare wall, there were bookcases of various heights, sizes and descriptions—even in the kitchen. The wall space not covered in books was covered with African masks, Navaho weaving, and prints that

ranged from wildly abstract to surprisingly senti-
mental.

Devon was not sure why it worked as well as it did,
but the room had sensation, feeling. It both invited
her to sit and be comfortable, and to explore. It was
both cozy and stimulating—a pleasant contradiction,
something very like the man in front of her.

She sank onto the sofa. "This is surprising."

"Is it?"

"It's a warm room," she explained.

"And I'm not a warm man?"

Warm? Warm was a nice comfortable word, and
went with nice comfortable things. Grey was either
ice cold—or red hot. And never comfortable.

"No, warm is not a word I would use to describe
you."

He moved into the kitchen, and she turned and sat
sideways on the sofa so she could still see him. She
liked the way he moved around his kitchen—with the
certainty of someone who used their kitchen a great
deal, and enjoyed it.

"You cook," she guessed.

He looked up at her in mild surprise. "Only when
I have a few hours that I can devote to it. Perhaps
you're in the wrong profession, Ms. Detective."

She didn't smile. For some reason she found it disturbing that he enjoyed gourmet cooking. Perhaps
because she couldn't imagine putting any kind of time
or effort into cooking, and then eating alone. Who
sat across that sturdy, scarred table from him? Did
he cover it with lace? Did he light candles?

"Hot chocolate," he said when he rejoined her.

She took the heavy mug from him and sipped it.
Ambrosia!

"This isn't like any hot chocolate I've ever tasted before," she commented.

"I use a mint-flavored chocolate, and a touch of coffee, and a touch of whipped cream."

How was it that a few hours ago she had doubted she would ever feel safe or happy again, and now she felt as safe and as happy as she ever had?

"What word would you use to describe me?" Grey asked suddenly.

The question took her off guard, but she studied him solemnly. "Enigmatic. Intriguing. Cynical. With a little dangerous thrown in."

"I'm not dangerous," he said softly.

"You are to me," she said huskily. "Very dangerous." That was the three glasses of wine talking, forcing her guard down, just as he had predicted! To think that mere seconds ago she had felt safe! But not now, with those ash-colored eyes resting on her so intently. It occurred to her that he looked relaxed, a quietness of spirit about him that she hadn't seen before. Perhaps that his job didn't allow him. So this was his sanctuary, the place where he could leave his job outside the door.

"What makes me dangerous to you?" His voice was a sensuous growl.

"Seeing you like this. Seeing you relaxed, and in your own element instead of mine, or my father's. Seeing you without your job wrapped around you like a cloak."

"And why is that so dangerous?" he pressed.

"Oh, Grey, stop it!" She shifted her eyes from his, and pretended avid interest in the window that looked out on to the street. "It's been there between us since the moment we met, and it's not going to go away."

Wine talking, dammit. *In vino veritas.* In wine, there is truth.

"Yes," he agreed, and her eyes flew back to his face.

She could feel the sensuality rolling off him, and unconsciously she leaned toward him, her lips parting, her eyes drooping.

"Don't, Devon," he said warningly.

"Don't what?" Her voice snapped, and so did her relaxed spine. She sat straight up and stared at him defiantly.

"We've already covered this ground tonight. Don't tempt me with those beautiful kissable rosebud lips."

"What would you have me do? Put them in my bag?"

Her awkward attempt at humor did not dispel the thickening atmosphere between them any more than his words had.

"You know I can't, Devon."

She recoiled from him as if he had hit her. Damn him and his job! "Yes, I know. Dan told me that it was against your rules to get involved with someone you've been assigned to work with. How commendable!"

He swore softly. "If I worried about the rules, you sure as hell wouldn't be sitting here right now."

Her eyes widened. "Then what are you worried about?"

"You. I already told you I'm not interested in vulnerable young maidens—no matter how appealing I find them. You're an appealing woman, Devon, spirited, intriguing, beautiful. And definitely off limits."

"I happen to be an adult, capable of making my own decisions, and living with the consequences."

"Devon, you don't even know what you want. One minute you're giving off siren signals and the next you're as prim as a freshly picked flower."

"I already told you what I want for tonight," she said stiffly, her wine-induced brazenness fading quickly. "I've had my Italian feast, and now I want to sleep—alone."

"Fine. You can have my bed—it's right down the hall."

"I don't want to sleep in your bed," she said, far too quickly. God, no! Not with his sheets and his scent surrounding her, with her head touching the same pillow his head touched, with her skin rubbing the same places his skin rubbed.

Grey frowned. "Are you sure? It's the more comfortable——"

"I already told you I find you rather dangerous," she told him crisply, trying to save a little of her pride. "I wouldn't want you making a wrong turn in the middle of the night after a nocturnal visit to the bathroom."

"Is that the way you see me as dangerous? I might stumble into you in the middle of the night and not be able to control myself?"

"Yes," she lied.

He looked both amused and relieved. "The couch has a hide-a-bed in it."

"Perfect!"

"I'll dig up something you can have for pajamas. Er—you can have the bathroom first. I think there's an unopened toothbrush in the top drawer of the vanity."

He entertained *guests* often enough to keep an extra toothbrush? Well, she shouldn't find that very surprising. She should be thanking her lucky stars that she wasn't about to become one of his conquests, despite her three glasses of wine, and the reckless words that had come out of her mouth.

"Do you let them keep the toothbrush?" she asked sweetly.

"Huh? Who?"

"As a kind of souvenir," she continued rashly.

Understanding dawned in his eyes. "I'm not that kind of man. My brother occasionally stays here overnight when he's had a hard day and doesn't want to commute back to his house. I keep a toothbrush for him—not that it's any of your business."

"Oh."

"Not that it's any of your business," Grey continued, his voice hard, "but I don't have any more respect for a man who sleeps around than for a woman who does it."

"Oh."

"Not that it's any of your business, but I happen to feel some pretty deep feelings should be involved before a man and a woman make the decision to become intimate. Emphasis on decision rather than accident."

Devon was blushing now.

He glared at her, stomped out of the room, and came back a moment later. He flung a T-shirt at her.

"I don't keep a full selection of nightwear, to complement my toothbrushes," he said sarcastically. "But it's clean."

"Grey, I'm sorry."

"Sorry?" he said, his eyes glinting dangerously.

"It's your own fault. You've never denied being a ladies' man before. In fact, you may have encouraged me to think that."

"Devon, I guess at some point I entertained the rather foolish notion that you were catching on to what I was really like, just as at some point I started to catch on to you."

"You did not," she contradicted.

"Sure I did. I know you use that touch-me-not tone of voice whenever you're feeling the most vulnerable." Wordlessly he tossed the cushions off the sofa and yanked out the bed. It was already made. Without so much as a glance at her, he turned and walked away. His bedroom door closed with a slam.

Hurriedly Devon went into the bathroom. The toothbrush was exactly where he had said it would be, a utilitarian black—exactly the type of toothbrush one stocked for a brother.

She took off her clothes, then pulled his T-shirt over her head. She looked at herself in the full-length mirror. The shoulders fell nearly to her elbows and it ended mid-thigh. It was dark blue and said "Renegades, Senior Men's League."

It was very evident she was naked beneath the shirt. It smelled of Grey because it had been laundered in the same kind of soap he used. She tore the T-shirt off and put her own clothes back on, uncaring of discomfort, uncaring if they got rumpled.

Feeling safely Victorian, she went and climbed into bed.

Alfonso was in the room. Devon could sense him moving in the shadows, watching her, a smile on his lips. She caught a movement in the shadows, a dark shape against darkness, lean and catlike. Alfonso. A glint of silver in the moon. He had a knife.

He came out of the shadows, his smile a leer, his eyes mad.

He raised the knife over his head and plunged it downward.

Her scream ripped through the room, and she awoke shaking and sobbing. Where was she? The room was black and unfamiliar. She desperately wanted a light on, but was too frightened to move.

She heard a crash, and splintering glass, and another scream escaped her. Her heart raced yet more. Was Alfonso really in here? Had she heard him coming in and the noises registered in her dreams?

"Devon?"

The hall light flicked on. Grey came toward her, wearing only pajama bottoms, blinking sleep from his eyes.

"Devon, what's going on?"

Her eyes fastened on his chest. It was broad and deep, the color of bronze. Thick, dark hair matted it. "I don't know," she stammered, disconcerted by his state of undress. "I think it was a dream." She looked again at his chest. Or maybe *this* was the dream. "I heard glass breaking—I'm sure that was real. Do you think Alfonso——"

Grey settled on the bed. It creaked under his weight. Her voice dried up; he was disconcertingly close. She could see that an occasional thread of pure silver glinted in that dark tangle on his chest.

"When you screamed, I jumped out of bed and started groping around for the lamp beside my bed," he said. "I broke it. Alfonso isn't here, Devon—he doesn't know where I live, and even if he did, he wouldn't come here. Do you understand?"

She did. Alfonso would not take on Grey. That had been evident from their first meeting. How did a man develop this quality of... of strength and confidence that made others instinctively respect him? Even somebody as irrational as Alfonso understood that Grey was not a man to be messed with. It was one thing to throw a rock through a window, one thing to write hate letters to a powerless woman. It would be quite another to beard the lion in his den.

The feeling of safety seeped back into her. A contented sigh escaped her. She liked having Grey this close—close enough that she could reach out and touch the silk-sheathed muscle of his arm, or his shoulder, if she wanted to.

"It was just a dream," he told her.

She wanted to. She didn't. He turned slightly and she noticed he was holding his left hand up gingerly, bent at the elbow like a doctor getting ready to glove. She saw the blood dripping down it.

"Oh, Grey!" She was fully awake now.

"It's just a scratch. I did it when I broke the lamp."

She reached across him to look. Her breasts brushed the hard expanse of his chest. She pulled marginally back and pretended not to notice, though it was pretty hard to ignore the jolt that shot through her from head to toe.

She took his arm firmly and forced his hand down. His skin felt alive beneath her fingertips, warm and resilient. Firmly she brought herself back on track and inspected the wound. It was more than a scratch. "Where are your medical supplies?" she asked.

"Just go back to sleep," he ordered. "I'll look after it." Had he noticed her reaction to the brief, forbidden contact with him? Or was it his own reaction that was making him so testy?

"You are the most stubborn human being I have ever come across!" she said crossly.

"Do you ever think we might make a good match?" His guard came down, and he grinned.

Devon ducked her head. That very thought had been occurring to her with unsettling frequency lately. She did not like the way he said it, as if it were the world's grandest joke.

"Where are the medical supplies?" she asked again, her voice no-nonsense.

"In the medicine chest in the bathroom, but really, Devon—— "

"Oh, shut up, Grey! For once in your life, just shut up!"

His mouth closed with a snap. He looked exactly the way one of her kids did when they were chastened. Hiding a smile, she went and fetched the supplies. She came back and sat on the bed beside him, taking his ripped hand on to her lap, and looking at it fairly clinically considering all the things going on inside her.

"You're getting blood all over you," he commented carefully, as if he was uncertain whether he was allowed to speak yet.

"It doesn't matter," she said lightly. "You've got some fragments of glass in there, so I'm just going to use the tweezers to pluck them out. Then I'll cleanse the wound with this alcohol and bandage it. It will hurt a bit, but I'll be done in no time."

She could feel his intent gaze on her face as she leaned over him. She knew the exact moment his gaze trailed lower and she prayed any physical reaction she was having to his nearness had died down. As uncomfortable as she was, she concentrated on what she was doing.

Finally she had the wound cleaned and dressed.

"Nice job," he commented, inspecting it carefully.

"You don't have a room full of accident-prone kindergarten kids without learning a thing or two," she assured him.

He laughed. "I thought I recognized your technique! Reassuring me by telling me exactly what was going to happen, and how it would feel, and how long it would take." His features sobered. "You're good with those kids, Devon—really good. Years from now they'll be giving the world back some of the gifts you've given them."

She flung back her hair and looked at him. She didn't think he'd ever given her a compliment before. Oh, he'd said she was attractive, but after all, that was what you were born with, the luck of the draw.

This was something quite different—an indication, however small, that he did not entirely buy his professed estimation of her as shallow and superficial. He'd said, earlier, that he was beginning to see who she really was. But was this what it took to make him say it? To coax a few soft words from him? His nearly bleeding to death in the middle of the night?

"Thank you." She didn't know what else to say.

"Well," he said awkwardly, "if you're all right, I'll head back to bed."

"Please don't go," she said softly. Her boldness took even her by surprise. But it was take a chance, or face the aching loneliness of the night by herself. "I won't go back to sleep for a while—not now. And neither will you."

Grey hesitated and she could see the struggle in his features. But once again he showed he was more vulnerable here on his own ground. Less inclined to be a Government agent and more inclined to be just human. Also it was the middle of the night. He was tired. And he'd been hurt. He probably didn't have the energy to maintain his customary professionalism.

Devon felt a rich sigh of contentment within her when he settled his naked back against the pillows. She stifled it.

"Okay," he said, "shoot."

"Shoot?" she queried.

"Well, you might as well tell me your life story since you have me here."

She laughed. "You know my life story. It's all in your little file."

"No, it isn't. That file doesn't have any of the important things, like your favorite color, or your favorite flower, or the name of the first boy you had a crush on."

"Purple. Hyacinth, because they smell like heaven. And George Dewbodey, the gardener's son at my first private school." She smiled. "He was the only boy around. I wonder how it felt to be ten and have six hundred small girls in love with you?"

"Miserable," Grey guessed. "Quite different from if you were twenty and had six hundred not so small girls in love with you. Did you like private schools, Devon?"

"I hated them," she admitted.

"Hm, somehow I guessed that. I can't picture you doing particularly well in a highly structured environment. I can't picture rules and Devon Paige getting on very well."

"I did fine at boarding school. My rebellion seems to have started later in life." *Like the day I met you.* "But I would have given my right arm to go to day school. It was just that my father has always had this thing——"

"Ah, yes, Uncle Charlie."

"How did you know?" she asked, taken aback.

"When you escaped my clutches I heard the whole story. I understand your need for independence, Devon, but I understood him too. Something like that leaves a mark on people."

"Goodness! It was fifty years ago, and the kidnappers never harmed a hair on Uncle Charlie's head."

"It doesn't matter. Your father was just a child, and he remembers his fear and helplessness with a child's clarity. His terror is real, Devon. Uncle Charlie was probably less harmed by the whole incident than the rest of the family because he knew what was going on, and wasn't left for three days to contemplate the worst. Nowadays the whole family could probably get psychiatric help to deal with something like that, but back then that's not what happened. Your father's been scarred by that incident. It makes him feel marginally safer to try and control you."

"Control is a mild word for what he gets up to," said Devon wryly. "When I first moved out, I had him over for dinner at my apartment. I was so proud and happy about how well I was doing on my own. The next morning I woke up to find steel grates going over my windows and a doorman installed. It was awful!''

"I know," said Grey. "He told me about it."

"Did he? He usually has the good grace to be embarrassed."

"He loves you, Devon. And you can handle him. You're a big girl now, and it's time to give him another chance."

She smiled. "You're a mind reader on top of everything else, are you? I've been thinking that for some time." She turned to him. "Did you know that at first I thought maybe he'd written those notes himself?"

"After I talked with him, I guessed that might be why you insisted on treating the whole thing like a game," said Grey.

"I don't feel that it's a game any more," she said softly. She moved marginally closer to him, and he shifted away.

"I'd better go to bed now," he stated flatly.

"I wish you wouldn't."

"What do you want from me, Devon?" he asked softly, a note of exquisite agony deepening the timbre of his voice.

"What do you think I want?"

"You want to know how it's supposed to be between a man and a woman. You want to release the volcanic passion that's built in you for years. You want to taste a man's sweat, and feel the naked hardness of his muscles. You want to be kissed and caressed to near madness——"

She gasped. She stared at him, and could feel the uncomfortable fire creeping up her neck.

"Isn't that what you want, Devon?" he asked harshly.

"No," she croaked, finally, unconvincingly.

"Well, if that's not what you want, you'd better kick me out of your bed."

"I don't see any ball and chain keeping you here."

"No?" he growled. He reached for her, and despite the unfathomable anger he was gentle. "What do you call this?" He touched her hair. "And this? And this?" His fingers traced her eyes, the arch of her cheek, the tender curve of her mouth. "Chains," he whispered raggedly. "They come in all shapes and sizes. Most chains don't even look like chains."

Devon knew about those kinds of chains. About a wanting without reason that haunted a person's very soul, that went to bed with them at night and got up with them in the morning. She wanted Grey, and he wanted her. Was it not a simple exchange? A giving of gifts? With no price tags, with no crippling request for a tomorrow he had not offered and could not promise her? With no expectations?

Tonight she could be free. She could break free of the shackles of wanting without having, until that wanting had become a deep and burning obsession that made her its prisoner. Tonight she could be free.

They could travel together, soaring above the bonds of earth. They could accept tonight, as a gift from the gods, that had no guarantees, that entered lives for moments, or days, or lifetimes, but gave no promises—except this one. That all who rose to this challenge would be changed for it. Perhaps they could not hold on to the person, or the feeling, for all time, but they would always have the gift of travelling for a time in a magic place—a place of mystery and majesty that was beyond human attempts to tame it, to capture it.

Am I courageous enough to embrace this thing within me that's wild and tender and that offers no guarantees? she asked herself.

The answer came swiftly. She touched him, as she had been wanting to touch him since he had joined her on the bed, as she had been wanting to touch him for days. She laid her white hand against the bronze of his chest, and stared at it. She moved it, slowly as if in a dream, down to the hard plane of his stomach, and up to the pebble-hard peak of his nipple.

"God, Devon," he rasped, "do you know what you're doing?"

"Yes." She rolled over on top of him, pressed her body against his, wrapped her arms around the solidness of his chest, and nestled her head in the hollow of his shoulders. "I want you," she whispered, and the tears streamed silently down her cheeks.

Grey stiffened beneath her. He was silent, and she could feel the raging struggle in his tension, and then his surrender. His body relaxed beneath her, and his hands moved tenderly to the tendrils of her hair.

"Oh, Devon, you've picked the wrong man to give yourself to."

"Picked?" She laughed, softly and with rich contentment. "Grey, we don't *pick*. Would we have such an enduring story as *Romeo and Juliet* if we picked? If we picked, do you really think the King of England would have chosen an American divorcée? The fates pick, and we're asked only if we have the courage to abide by their choice."

"Devon, I can't let you——"

She laughed, a low throaty chuckle. All these weeks she had marveled at his control, been intimidated by his power. And now she walked the sacred ground that a million women had walked before her. His power and his control had seemed formidable obstacles, insurmountable. And now she knew that his walls would crumble like dust before the gentlest whisper of invitation from her lips.

She kissed him. Tenderly. With welcome. And promise.

He groaned—and in that low sound that came from the bottom of his belly he told her. He was defeated, utterly lost. Hers.

She took his lower lip gently between her teeth and nipped it, felt his quick intake of breath, felt his arms tighten around her.

"Devon," he whispered, as his tongue traced the delicate outline of her ear. "Devon."

His lips moved, moist and heated, down the slender column of her throat, and goose bumps rose in their wake. She tingled against him, feeling as though her quaking was outside her and inside her too. The volcano he had said she was.

It began like this, with a deep inner trembling and a slow inching up of the thermostat. He was in no hurry. His lips lingered here and there, paying homage to the softness of her skin. Tasting her, touching her, testing her.

Grey picked her up with awe-inspiring ease, walked down a short hall to his bedroom, entered it and slammed the door behind him.

CHAPTER NINE

GREY set her down gently in the center of his bedroom floor. The light from the hall spilled over his broad shoulder.

"Take off your clothes," he commanded, his voice soft, but uncompromising.

Devon had always been shy of her body, self-conscious. She had never skinny-dipped when the rest of the kids at camp had skinny dipped, she had never confidently stripped in the gym shower room during high school. It occurred to her that no one in her entire life had seen her completely unclothed.

And yet this felt beautifully, astonishingly right. This shyness melted before the desire that burned like a slow fire through the darkening gray of his eyes.

As she stood there, in the half light, bathed in gold, her fingers found the buttons of her blouse. Without taking her eyes from his, she taunted him. With infinite and slow care she slipped each of the buttons from their holes. When the blouse fell open she tossed back her head and slipped her hand inside, carelessly, appreciatively, ran her hand from her breastbone to her belly.

She heard his sharp intake of breath, lowered her head to gaze at him through desire-narrowed eyes. She eased one arm out of a sleeve, traced the bare flesh of her arm and shoulder with her fingertips, and then eased out her other arm. The blouse whispered to the floor, and lay at her feet in a white puddle.

She wore one of those dainty white camisoles that she had bought that day several weeks ago, so shortly after Grey had first entered her life. Had she known, even then? In some far-off place in her mind, had she known even then that this night would be the natural culmination of their relationship? The camisole was fine silk, more film than fabric.

She watched his eyes darken to a shade approaching black, and allowed herself a small smile, then stretched languorously, her arms over her head, thrusting her breasts against the softness of the fabric so that it molded to her.

"God, Devon," he said hoarsely. He took a step toward her, but she twirled away, an unselfconscious night nymph, wanting to play with his senses a while longer. He stopped, and it satisfied her to see how much control it took for him to stop.

She rested her fingers on the top fastening of her button down skirt, changed her mind, and reached up to slowly drop one of the spaghetti straps of her camisole. Then she let her hands drop again, and with a deliberation she knew he found maddening she carefully undid the top three buttons of her skirt. She stood, frozen for a moment, her eyes wickedly wanton on his face. Then she let the skirt go and it swirled softly to her feet.

A harsh sound of suffering came from deep down in Grey's throat. The panties matched the camisole. Silk, lace-edged, high-cut. A white, lace-edged garter held up her stockings and she leaned over, ever so casually, unfastened one snap at a time, and peeled the stockings off the long, smooth length of her leg.

A part of her was now nearly giddy. Where had this seductress come from? From the look on Grey's face, he had got a little more than he bargained for.

She peeled off her other stocking with the same lazy pretense of lack of caring, straightened and looked at him. "Your turn," she commanded huskily.

She saw immediately that two could play her taunting, teasing game, because with his eyes fastened on her face, and, his mouth unsmiling, he unfastened the drawstring on his pajama bottoms with so much care that she could feel herself begin to tremble from her effort not to go and speed things along their way with her own fingers.

He saw her leaning unconsciously toward him, but his faint acknowledging smile made her jerk back. Like a bud unfolding to its full majesty in time-lapse photography, he stripped off the pants and stood before her. Still. Entirely still. Carved in rock. A spark of laughter lit his eyes at the hunger she could not hide as she drank in the glory of his hard, perfect body.

She actually ached to touch him—to see if the hard perfect cut of his pectorals was flesh or stone, to trace the sinewy mounds of gold-washed biceps with reverent, curious, seeking fingers. To run her questing hands through the hint of hair that formed a hard arrow over the flat concave of his belly.

She gulped, her mouth dry, her breathing oddly rapid. He still didn't move, just stood there with a complete lack of self-consciousness. Proudly and majestically male. A knowing glitter in his eyes telling her he knew exactly the effect he was having on her senses.

After a long moment, she let her eyes drift back up to his face. A trickle of sweat curled down the side of his forehead, followed the line of his jaw. He made no attempt to brush it away.

"Grey," she whimpered, and reached her hands over her head.

He crossed the distance between them in one long, silent stride. With sure hands, he took the hem of her camisole and tugged it up over her head. For a moment he stood frozen, the camisole limp, impossibly white and fragile against the dark strength of his hand. And then he dropped it carelessly onto the floor and his eyes drank in the ripeness of her freed breasts.

Devon felt her only moment of self-consciousness then. His expression was awed, reverent, gentle. She started to lower her arms, to cover herself, to escape from the intensity of his expression.

But she was stilled by the easy strength of his hands, and his eyes met hers.

"Devon, you're so beautiful. So incredibly beautiful."

He lowered her arms to her sides and held them captive there, and dropped his head over her breast.

Devon gasped with astonished pleasure as his lips, heated and moist, captured the tip of her breast. He let go of her hands, sure now that she was his captive. And she grasped him, dug her fingernails mindlessly into the silk-sheathed iron of his shoulder, as she pulled him closer.

He picked her up, tossed her on the bed, looked down at her sprawled before him, with merciless passion darkening his eyes to pitch.

"Grey, please," she whispered, holding out her hands to him. "Please!"

He came down on top of her and his weight felt glorious. His hardness crushed her softness, melding it to fit the ruthless contours of his muscular body. His lips, fire, turned her to the liquid that would quench him, put him out.

He touched her, kissed her, stroked her, posessively, with infinite knowing.

She quivered below him, glorying in the feel of his hard flesh, tasting the salt of his sweat on her lips and savoring it. Her body ached with age-old yearning, cried out for the fulfillment it had never attained.

"Devon!"

Her eyes flew open at the soft urgency in his voice; her body protested his sudden stillness.

"Love," he touched her cheek with the palm of his hand, "it isn't always good the first time. I'll be gentle. I promise you."

She nodded, his tenderness burning through her mind, before he hurtled her over the abyss into the startling brilliance of sensation that was the center of her desire.

"Are you all right? Are you all right? Are you all right?" His voice coming from a million miles away, muted by the thundering surf of some storm-tossed inner sea.

She opened her eyes, smiled at the concern etched into his rugged, familiar face. She cupped his cheek in her palm, and smiled.

"Oh, Grey, I'm fine. I'm just fine."

"Tigress," he growled. "Beautiful, enchanting, wild, wicked tigress."

"Warrior," she answered him back. "Majestic, strong, gloriously proud warrior."

"No, not a warrior. Sometimes—but not tonight. Tonight—— " he kissed her in a place she had never dreamed of being kissed, and his lips felt like a brand "—I am your servant."

She awoke washed in the golden light of the morning sunshine that was streaming through the rounded arch of his bedroom window. She stretched sleepily, savoring the feeling of lazy contentment, fulfillment, that satiated her being. She cuddled deeper under the quilt, appreciating its scent and its softness, smiling at how rumpled it was. She let her eyes rove the room, taking in the details that she had not noticed the night before. A masculine room, dominated by the four-poster bed that was so large she felt small lying in it.

She turned to Grey, and her heart leapt into her throat. Had she really believed she could do this and walk away afterward? Had she really believed that she would be free of her feelings for him by giving in to her desire? Had she really been naive enough to believe that was all there was to her feelings for Grey?

Still, she felt no regret. None. And no anxiety.

She touched her lips to the skin of his upper arm. It tasted faintly of salt. It smelled more heavenly than hyacinth. She ran her tongue from his shoulder to his elbow—and laughed when strong arms reached over and she found herself sprawled on top of his chest, looking into his eyes that were very much awake.

"Goot mornink," she said in her best imitation of a Russian accent. She blinked her eyes at him. "Do I knowink all your secrets yet?"

"Uh-uh," he said, his gray eyes smoldering, his chiseled lips twisting into a wicked smile. "I haven't begun to show you my secrets. Like this one, for instance."

His cheeks and chin had become whisker-shadowed through the night, and he scraped that rough texture— with incredible gentleness—over the peaks of her delicate breasts.

She gasped, then shuddered with pleasure. "Oh, my God, Grey!"

"Or this one." He flipped her over in one adept motion and was on top of her, pushed her hair back, and found her ear with his tongue.

"Grey——" she muttered a little desperately. Who would have guessed *ears* could be such a sensual center of the body?

"Or this one," he growled . . .

The phone rang. Its shrillness was like a physical scratch across the sensitised surface of her skin.

Grey lifted his head. "Aw, damn!"

"Don't answer it," she suggested throatily.

He rolled off of her. "I have to answer it."

She rolled with him. "No, you don't."

"Temptress!" But he put her gently away from him, and got up.

"You'll be sorry," she told him. "It's probably someone selling newspaper subscriptions."

"I doubt it." He removed his pajama pants from a tangle of clothes on the floor and tugged them on.

Devon watched him, astounded by the beauty of his body, shivering with their remembered intimacy. She wished the phone would stop ringing, but it didn't. She felt cheated when he walked out of the room.

She listened to him answer the phone. She could hear the low rumble of his voice but not the words. After a while she gave up hoping he would be right back. The sound of him talking lulled her back to sleep.

When she awoke again she was still in the big bed alone. The sun was pitching in the window at a steep angle. Where on earth was Grey? The smell of coffee drifted in to her, and she swung her feet out of the bed. She looked at the tangle of clothing on the floor and opted for one of his white dress shirts that was draped over the back of a chair instead. Feeling slightly guilty, like a child stealing a cookie, she put it to her nose and breathed deeply of his scent. She slipped it on and did up the buttons, then went and had a look at herself in the full-length mirror behind his closet door.

She smiled with delight. She looked wildly alluring, her hair a-tangle, her eyes smudge pots that glowed with a wicked new knowledge, her lips faintly bruised, her cheeks flying flags of high color. The shirt clung to her breasts and its tails touched her thigh. She rolled up the sleeves, hesitated, then undid two of the shirt's top buttons and went out of his bedroom.

Her eager smile turned to a frown. Grey was behind the low counter that separated his kitchen area from the rest of his apartment, fully dressed.

She had been anticipating seeing him barefoot, barechested, still in those low-slung pajamas. But he was dressed in gray pants, a white shirt, and a gray tie. His jacket was draped over the back of one of the dining-room chairs. Work clothes.

He looked up and froze. His eyes touched her with hot remembrance, and came to rest appreciatively on the long, tanned length of her leg poking out from under his shirt. Last night's passion lit his eyes.

And then was doused.

"That shirt never looked that great on me," he commented, but his voice didn't carry the attempt at lightness.

Devon sat down at one of the high stools on the other side of the counter. "I thought you'd come back to bed." She tried to sound uncaring. Her tone was no lighter than his had been. She plucked a muffin from a basket and concentrated on that instead of on his eyes.

"Something's come up. Dan Nelligan's taking over today—he'll be here in a few minutes. Coffee's ready."

She felt frozen to her stool. *I'm leaving you. Coffee's ready.* God, how could he be so hard? How could he just leave behind last night without a trace of its tenderness, without bringing some small piece of it into today?

But hadn't she always known he was hard? How much of last night had been her own desperate need? To be fulfilled, to give imaginary traits of tenderness to the man who fulfilled her in order to salve her own conscience.

But no, she had not imagined his tenderness. The tenderness in his hands and his lips, and in lovemaking that had been so much more than she had ever imagined lovemaking could be.

She could feel the heat creeping into her face, even as she could feel the tears creeping into her eyes. She got up swiftly and went into the kitchen. She brushed by him and took an earthenware mug from where it was hanging from a hook underneath his cupboard. She filled her cup with coffee and took a long steadying sip before she felt she could return to her chair.

Absurdly, Dan Nelligan was associated in her head with Grey's days off, and that was what she asked him.

"Is it your day off?" *Don't you want to spend it with me?*

He gave her a sharp, incredulous look, as if he could not believe how ridiculous she was.

"I don't dress like this on my day off," he told her brusquely. A softness slipped into his tone. "If it was my day off do you think anything on heaven or earth could have moved me from that bed?"

"I don't know how you spend your days off." She bit into her muffin. "I don't know very much about you."

"That's a hell of a thing to say!"

"It's a hell of a thing to leave the woman you've just loved."

"I don't have a choice, Devon."

"Tell me, Grey, was last night an *accident* or a *choice*?"

He hesitated. "A bit of both, I guess. Now, would you kindly get dressed before Nelligan shows up?"

Devon stared at him in utter disbelief, and his form swam before her eyes. She whirled and ran back into the bedroom.

She was showered and dressed when he came in later. She couldn't bear to put her crumpled clothes back on and had borrowed some of his. She was wearing a sweatshirt and a pair of his jeans, rolled up and severely belted. But that mysterious glow was still in her cheeks and her eyes, and she could have been wearing a sackcloth and still looked as utterly sensual as she had ever looked. She didn't turn away from the mirror where she stood brushing her hair.

She could see the moment Grey looked at her that he found her intoxicatingly sexy too. He came up behind her, and her hand stilled as she looked at his reflection towering over her shoulder.

"I'm sorry," he said, and planted a light kiss on her neck. "I've got a lot on my mind this morning."

"Me too," she said coldly. Imagine being beguiling and sexy for the first time in your life, and your man finding you so resistible. What a waste! And maybe she would do better not to even think of him as her man. No promises had passed between them.

"Nelligan's here already." He turned away from her and went over to a low bureau against another wall.

"Well, I'm all dressed, so he won't know that you broke your code of ethics, if that's what you're worried about."

Grey turned and looked at her oddly. "I never gave a thought to what he might think of *me*."

She noticed then what he was doing. He shrugged a big shoulder into the shoulder holster. He kept his back to her, but she heard the clicks, and knew instinctively that he was checking the chambers on his weapon. A moment later he slid it into the holster.

"Where are you going?" she asked, a premonition of danger running up and down her spine. The last time she had felt danger this acutely, a gray-eyed stranger had been eyeing her from the other side of her father's library. She had been right that time! She suddenly felt more frightened than she had ever been in her life.

"Out." He started to walk toward the door, but she blocked him with her body, dug her fingernails deep into his arm.

"Don't go," she pleaded. "Grey, please don't go!"

"Devon," he detached her arm gently, "I don't want to leave you like this. I want to climb back into that bed and love the world away as much as you do. But I can't. I have work to do, and it won't wait."

"Please tell me," she whispered. "Please tell me what's so important. Please don't shut me out of your world, Grey. That would be the only thing that would make it unbearable to me."

He hesitated, staring down at her. Something crept into the coolness in his eyes. Some small tenderness, a reluctant memory of last night chased the professional mask from his face. He was suddenly back in the here and now, instead of thinking about whatever it was that had brought that preoccupied crease to his brow.

His shoulders heaved with a defeated sigh. "They've got Alfonso. He's holed up in a downtown tenement. That dumb kid got his hands on a gun. And he's taken two hostages."

Devon felt the blood drain from her face. She wanted to tell him not to go, but couldn't. It was his job to go. It was a part of him to go.

But if he hurt Alfonso how could she ever live with that? Somewhere, Grey might have hurt someone—that was one of the hazards of a job like his. But it would have been a faceless criminal who smuggled drugs or something. She could live with that.

But Alfonso was not faceless, and, even though he had betrayed her trust in him, she could not bear the thought of him being violently hurt, perhaps even dying—not at Grey's hand. He was little more than a child, a young man deranged by his environment. A victim as much as a criminal.

"Don't hurt Alfonso." It came out a whisper of despair, the tears gathering in her eyes and trickling down her cheeks as she looked imploringly up at him.

"That's exactly why I'm going," he told her grimly. "To try and keep that mixed-up, young punk from getting himself killed." He touched her cheek, his eyes puzzled on her face. "You really don't know me at all, do you?"

She felt relief sweep her. "Grey, I'm starting to know you. I know you well enough to know I can't ask you not to go." She hesitated, then continued, her voice husky with emotion. "But not in any of the ways that count," she whispered. "What's your favorite color? Your favorite flower? What was the name of the first girl you had a crush on?"

The recrimination left his eyes. "Red," he answered solemnly. "Lilacs. Wilma."

And then he whirled, and was gone.

She spent several minutes composing herself before she went out into the apartment. Dan Nelligan was sprawled out on the couch, in his shirtsleeves, wearing an ugly shoulder holster just like Grey's. He sipped a cup of coffee.

"Hi there." If he in any way found this situation awkward he certainly managed not to show it. He picked up the channel changer. "Which do you prefer? Morning cartoons or a re-run of last night's Dodgers game?"

"It doesn't matter to me," she said. She felt as if she was moving in a dream—a very bad dream. She went and got herself another cup of coffee, then sat down on a corner of the couch and took a sip. Grey made good coffee. She had so many things to learn about him, so many things to know.

They had parted on good terms, but she sensed that any hope for the future depended on what happened today—not to him, but to her. Did she have the strength to handle this particular kind of stress?

"The Dodgers it is," said Dan, grinning at her. His grin faded at her expression.

"Look," he tried to reassure her uncomfortably, "Grey will be all right. He knows how to look after himself out there."

"You don't like to think about how scary it is," she guessed with sudden insight.

He looked rueful. "No, ma'am, I don't."

"Is Grey in danger?"

He hesitated, took in the stubborn set of her jaw, and sighed. "He's the only one who has any personal knowledge of Smithers. They've asked him to negotiate."

"Meaning?"

"Meaning he'll see if Smithers will trade his hostages for him. And then once he's inside——"

Devon closed her eyes. Was Grey crazy? Didn't he know it was Alfonso's jealousy of him that had brought this whole situation to a head to begin with? What would Alfonso do, alone with Grey in a room, when he was holding a gun? What would the heady sensation of power do to Alfonso, especially in the light of how intimidated he had been by Grey? Would that grudging respect he had for Grey hold any water at all when he was wielding a gun?

"Grey's negotiated hostages before," Dan told her. "He's not bad at it."

"Thank you," Devon said tightly. "That's very reassuring."

"He's my friend too," Dan said in a pained voice.

She looked at him, and realized how selfish she was being. It was in his face that he'd lost friends before, and would rather do anything than look at the possibility of losing another.

She took his hand. "I'm sorry. I just wanted you to say he was the greatest hostage negotiator in the world, that's all. Let's watch the Dodgers game."

Dan scanned her face. "You really love him, don't you?"

"Yes." The answer came quietly, with a calm certainty that took her by surprise. Yes, she loved him.

She had tried to call it different things. She had tried to explain her behavior in different ways. She had tried and tried and tried to outrun loving him. And failed. Never had acknowledging a failure brought her such a sense of peace, of rightness. She loved Grey. Nothing could change that—not even being afraid of loving him.

So, if this was a part of loving him, this waiting, and wondering, she would try to do it as bravely as she could. Oh, being a woman had not changed so very much over the centuries. Being a woman meant waiting for your man to come home, from slaying dragons and fighting wars and doing all those hard things that men were asked to do, and unhesitatingly did. But now she knew the truth. The true courage belonged to those who waited. To those who loved enough to accept the pain of waiting.

She remembered Grey talking about her father and her uncle Charlie, and saying her father had been the one traumatized most by Uncle Charlie's kidnapping, because he had been the one who waited. And now she was in that same position.

"I think he cares for you too," Dan commented slowly. "When he took that weekend off, and I replaced him, I found out he'd been offered the two-week leave that he was owed—as a peace offering from the Colonel, I guess. Grey had some reservations about the Colonel's plans for a dope bust. He didn't word his opinions very diplomatically, and wound up being kicked off the assignment, and landing on your doorstep. Unfortunately his reservations proved all too apt. Offering him his leave, after all, was probably as close as the Colonel could come to apologizing.

"But Grey wouldn't take it. And he wouldn't let Wilson anywhere near you, partly because Wilson is so inexperienced, but partly too because Wilson has such a big crush on you."

Devon managed a small laugh.

"Then he read me the riot act this morning. Called me an aging Romeo, told me the only thing I'd better lay my lips to in his house was a peanut butter sandwich and a cup of coffee."

Devon laughed again, shakily, appreciating the fact that Dan was trying to help her relax.

"Of course, he's always been kind of a nasty bastard," Dan went on. "I remember the time..."

In between pitches that neither of them were really watching, he regaled her with anecdotes of he and Grey's careers when they had intertwined.

"Yeah," he said, "he used to have quite a sense of humor. But he's changed over the last few years. A job like this takes its toll on a person. Grey's lonely, but he doesn't seem to think he can ask anyone to share his world. He thinks he's the only strong one, I guess. I think he's old-fashioned about women—thinks they need to be protected and cosseted, and never allowed a moment's worry. The right woman could probably change his mind.''

Devon closed her eyes. On one hand she felt hope. She might be strong enough to take on Grey and his stubborn belief system. Might. Today would tell. But that might also be the easy part. She shuddered at the thought of trying to convince Grey he was wrong about anything.

''We break in to this re-broadcast of last night's ball game to give an update on the hostage——''

Dan picked up the channel changer and switched it.

''Put it back,'' she ordered firmly.

He eyed her woefully, then did as he was told.

''...Trevor McGregor, live at the hostage site. We're getting only snatches of information from the SWAT team here, but it does appear that a new negotiator has arrived.''

The camera switched to a shot of Grey unfolding from his car, giving the cameraman a dirty look, then crouching and running closer to the roped-off apartment.

Devon stared at him, her throat dry. His face was absolutely calm, as if he had nothing to lose in being there. She watched as he held a huddled conference with several policemen in baseball caps and bullet-proof vests. Then she saw him taking off his own jacket and shrugging into a bullet-proof vest.

The voice-over droned on, ''We have been unable to confirm a name, but it appears the new negotiator is going to try and reopen communication with the hostage taker. Phone contact was lost early this morning, but both hostages have been seen at the window in the past hour.'' The announcer's voice was cut abruptly, and the disembodied sound of a voice coming over a bullhorn reached them.

"Alfonso, this is Grey Carmichael."

Could that tinny, harsh voice be the voice of the man who had whispered to her tenderly in the darkness of night?

"I'm coming in!"

"That's not negotiation!" she told him wildly, as if he could hear her. She was unheeding of the amused look Dan gave her. She waited, her very heart stopped, for Alfonso, whose shadow had appeared at a window, to yell at Grey to stay where he was.

Grey apparently waited too. And when nothing happened, he carefully put the bullhorn on top of a police cruiser and made a grave show of removing his own gun from the holster and setting it beside the bullhorn. He picked up the bullhorn again.

"I'm coming in—now. I'm unarmed."

She turned frantically. "Is he really? Unarmed?"

"Probably," said Dan tersely.

"Oh, for heaven's sake!" she muttered. "In movies they always have something hidden in their sock."

Dan started to laugh, took one look at her face, and obviously thought better of it.

"Oh, God," she said, her voice muffled by her clenched fists. "There he goes."

They both leaned forward to watch, as Grey strode calmly across the no-man's-land between the apartment and the police barricades, and disappeared inside the dark door.

CHAPTER TEN

"I SHOULD be the one there," Devon said frantically. To her horror, the baseball game came back on. She snatched the channel changer from Dan.

She flipped channels. "Dan, I should go there. I could talk to Alfonso. I think he'd listen to me."

"Forget it, honey. No one's going to let you within a mile of that building."

"I could talk to him over the phone. I——"

"He snipped the phone wires this morning."

"Dan, please——"

"Grey warned me you might try and talk me into taking you to the hostage site. Would you care to guess what he had to say on the subject?"

She gave a defeated sigh, threw her head against the back of the couch, and stared morosely at the ceiling. "No."

"Wise lady." He stared at the switching pictures on the TV. "Devon, it's his job. If your man was a teacher, or a tycoon, or a fireman, you wouldn't follow him to work."

"This is different. I'm involved in this." But she knew that wasn't quite true. She just wanted to be with him, near him. As if she could control what fate would throw his way today by the force of her will, by the puny power of her presence. And she realized she couldn't do that. Not with anyone—teacher, tycoon, fireman, law enforcement officer.

She put the TV back on the channel where the ball game was playing. If they had any hope for a future she would have to prove, to Grey and to herself, that she could recognize boundaries. Where he left off and she began. What was his to deal with in life and what was hers. What she could control, and what she could not.

She had always, despite her father's efforts to breed suspicion into her, believed that basically life was good, and now she would have to carry that faith into this new situation. Life was good. Love was good. Those beliefs were what gave the strength to face up to the bad with courage and resolve and calm.

She could do it too. Hold on to her dreams of how she would like it to be, of a safe and secure world for them—but then deal with the reality that today handed her with courage and calm.

If she was going to be worthy of being Grey's mate, she could not cling to him, or cry for him every time he went out of that door. If she was going to be worthy of being his mate, she had to believe he was the very best at doing what he did, and that everything that was in his power to do to protect himself, he would do. She recognized that in life there was always a point where personal power left off, and another mysterious and compelling force took over.

In this she found peace. She forced herself to get on with life. To watch television, and joke with Dan, and to look through Grey's books and magazines for something to read. She even started preparing the groundwork for an art project she thought her pupils would enjoy.

The news bulletins flashed intermittently through the morning and afternoon. Early in the afternoon the two hostages were released, and the camera followed them as they ran from the building. With the typical ruthlessness of the Press they were given absolutely no time to recover before the microphones were put under their noses.

Both of them, an elderly woman and a middle-aged man, seemed very collected as they described fragments of their ordeal.

"Grey Carmichael," said the elderly woman, "is like a guiding angel in there. Poor Alfie's a very mixed-up lad, but I think Grey will bring him around." Her complete capitulation to Grey's charms made Devon ruefully shake her head—did his masculine charisma *ever* quit?

The camera changed to the male hostage's viewpoint.

"The atmosphere reversed," the well-spoken man said, "as soon as Mr. Carmichael came into the room. It went from contained panic to controlled calm. He is in utter control of the situation. He had unbelievable resources of humor and patience. I have absolute confidence in him, and in his ability to manipulate a very touchy situation to a peaceful resolution. It was very evident to me that Mr. Smithers had a healthy respect for Mr. Carmichael, albeit a grudging one. I think this situation is very close to being concluded."

Devon felt her heart nearly stop with relief. Surely that meant that any second things would be over? She shared this hopeful thought with Dan.

"Don't count on it," he responded cautiously. "These things take a lot of time. It almost seems the more time they take, the more chance there is of a good outcome."

She felt her heart sink. If the released hostage had been wrong about how close things were to resolution, what else had he been wrong about? She fought a fresh surge of panic.

She had to believe in Grey. And she found she did. She forced herself to make some lunch for both of them, then talked Dan into coming out for a walk around Grey's quaint, quiet neighborhood. The tension eased and flowed back, eased and flowed back, but each time it came back with a little less force. If she was going to love this man successfully, she would have to detach herself from the danger of what he did. Live each moment he gave her for what it was— a gift, a celebration of life. And part of what made life such a spectacular adventure, after all, was its complete lack of guarantees.

When they came back in from their walk the early evening news was just starting.

"Our headline story tonight: the hostage taking is over. Also on tonight's news..."

Neither of them even made it to the couch. They jostled for positions side by side on the coffee table right in front of the TV and sat without breathing through an agony of commercials.

Finally the anchorman reappeared, his face so bland and unrevealing that Devon could have screamed.

"The hostage taking at the Valley Crest apartment complex is over. Only moments ago, negotiator Grey Carmichael, from the Federal Law Enforcement Agency——"

Devon closed her eyes. *Please, God, please.*

"—left the building with one Alfonso Smithers. We go to the scene."

Her eyes shot open.

The television picture, wobbling before her teary eyes, showed Grey, walking out of the apartment building. Grey's face was closed to the cameras—remote and without emotion. But her eyes, her lover's eyes, saw things others would not see: a hint of exhaustion underlying his brisk stride, a faint world-weariness shadowing his eyes.

A bittersweet victory, she guessed, with utter sadness. This was not one of those times that he had gained the rush of satisfaction from his job. She saw the compassion in the way Grey had wrapped his arm around Alfonso's thin shoulders, as if he was protecting him from the reality of the dozens of rifles trained on them.

Devon's eyes drifted to Alfonso. Tired confused tears ran down his face.

She hugged herself against the stab of pain that ripped through her as she remembered Alfonso at his best . . . playing with the children, learning something new and trying not to appear too pleased about it . . . so eager to be around her, to win moments of her attention.

How could she have missed the signs that he cared about her in such a different way than she had cared about him? How could she be so arrogant as not to see? Could she have prevented this tragic conclusion if she had been more sensitive, more open?

Alfonso, she told him inwardly, I'm sorry. But you've helped to make me a different person. Perhaps, in some way that's so hard to believe right now, this is exactly what both of us needed to happen. You to get the help you so desperately need, and me to learn to be more humble, more present to people, less sure of the lines of "station."

She watched the unfolding news report, showing recaps of the whole event, numbly, gauging her own sense of desolation. She had thought she would feel only joy. Several times today she had chased away negative thoughts by imagining herself and Dan dancing wildly around the room in celebration of this very news. Instead the tears raced down her cheeks even faster.

The news report switched back to the present just as Grey held up a hand as a circle of news teams tightened around them, shouldered his way wordlessly through to a police cruiser. He opened the door, helped Alfonso into the back, then climbed in beside him.

In the shadows of the car, she could see Alfonso bury his head in Grey's chest and cry. A moment later the police cruiser pulled away, lights flashing, but no sirens.

Dan turned down the sound and they sat side by side, a kind of relieved paralysis creeping over them. But no celebration. Not even smiles.

"I think," Devon said slowly, "I'm beginning to understand what a hard, hard thing it is you men do."

Dan let out a sigh. "It makes it harder if your sensitivity survives. Grey's got to be just exhausted. But he probably told the kid he'd help him—go through it with him, find him a lawyer."

"Well, then, that's what he'd have to do. A promise is a promise." Silently she thanked Grey for fulfilling the promise he had made to her the previous day. Though from what Dan said, maybe Grey would have done exactly the same thing with no prodding from her.

Dan grinned at her. "I would have probably made all kind of promises too—and tossed him to the wolves as soon as I was out that door! Grey cares about people. Even the ones on the wrong side. It's nice—but it destroys you."

"No, it doesn't," she murmured from the bottom of her heart. "It hasn't destroyed Grey at all. It's made him stronger, more alive—deeper. People are almost irresistibly attracted to Grey. In moments of jealousy I've blamed his male charm. But now I think it's something else altogether. People sense that he has a unique quality of integrity—an ability to feel for them and to care about them. He does that because he believes he's helping people, and if he ever loses that quality I don't think he could do this kind of work any more."

"Spoken like a woman in love," Dan teased her, but gently, and with respect. She realized he had come to respect her this afternoon, and she was grateful for this unspoken vote of confidence. She would need it.

She thought about the people milling around Grey at lunchtime at the school, drawn to him. Because it was so apparent that life had dealt him some pretty tough hands, and he still managed to care.

She could learn from a man like that. She would learn, for the rest of her life. All that was left to do was convince Grey to see things her way. She smiled, remembering the power she had realized, last night, finally, that she could wield over this powerful man.

"I guess you can go now," she said sweetly to Dan.

"Go?" he said with surprise. "I haven't been officially pulled——"

"Just go," she pleaded.

He looked at her eyes and smiled. "Sure. There are definite times when three would be a crowd!"

When Grey walked in, hours later, Devon had turned off all the lights to make his apartment seem deserted. She watched from the shadows as he paused in the doorway, and listened. She could see what he would never have allowed her to see—that he wanted her to be there.

She could tell by the way he paused in the doorway, like a man who had dared to hope. When he was greeted with silence, she could see the weariness in the set of his shoulders intensify. He didn't turn on the light, but he didn't have to; she could hear his bleakness in the uncharacteristic heaviness in his tread.

He flopped down in a chair, his exhaustion seeping out of him, tangible in the air around him. In the half-light coming in from the side window she studied the familiar planes of his face. So rugged. So fiercely independent. A face of great strength and great fortitude. The face of a man who had had to be too strong, who had needed, and had denied his own need. To come home to warmth and companionship and love. To come home to a woman who could take the hurts in his heart and do as woman had done for centuries—heal them with the love in her heart.

He leaned forward, his elbows on his knees, his face buried in the palms of his hands, experiencing some immensely personal moment of grief. She waited until it was over, until the shaking in his shoulders had subsided.

She felt to her soul the lonely landscape of the life he had led. She emerged from the shadows carrying a candlelit tray. On it were tall chilled glasses of fresh fruit juice, thick sandwiches, and a dish of fat strawberries. She was wearing one of his huge T-shirts, a red one, belted at her waist with a tie. Her feet were bare and her hair was loose, save for a sprig of lilac she had put in over her ear.

"Devon," he whispered, and, in his weariness, his relief and his abject vulnerability came through. He tried to cover it. "What are you doing here?" he asked gruffly.

"I thought you might need me."

"Well, I don't," he said harshly.

"Tonight," she said softly, ignoring his uninviting tone completely, and setting down her tray on the coffee table, "I am your servant." She knelt at his feet and started to take off his shoes.

Hands with no weariness in them at all spanned her waist and she felt herself being lifted onto his lap. She stared into the breathtaking darkness of his eyes.

"You don't know what you're doing," he warned her huskily.

"Yes, I do."

"Devon, if I have one more night like last night, I'll never be able to let you go. Do you understand that?"

"Yes, I do."

"No, you don't. You don't have a clue what you're letting yourself in for. I'm giving you a chance." He loosed his arms from her waist. "Go."

She sat very still, her eyes unwavering on his.

"Devon, I don't have the strength to fight you tonight."

"You're very strong," she said. "You've been fighting me for a long time."

"Don't unman me," he muttered, then sighed, and closed his eyes. "Yes, Devon, I've been fighting you for a long time. But I can't tonight. I have nothing left to fight you with."

She savored the irony of that. It was the job she felt so much unease about that had given her the moment she craved. His utter weakness.

"I'm staying," she said.

"Don't. Don't stay here for one more night, and then walk away from me."

She touched his face. "I won't, Grey," she whispered. "I'm staying—for good."

"No! Dammit, Devon, you don't know what this job can do to two people——"

"Don't you think I found out all about what your job is going to do to me this afternoon? I watched a blow-by-blow account of your heroics on television."

"Oh, hell! Dan should have had more sense——"

"Grey, listen to me. I was frightened. But I was also very, very proud of you. And very, very proud of me. I'm strong enough for a man like you."

"Devon," he said wearily, "I know how strong you are. And courageous. I watched you walk through that inner city every day as if you were sashaying down Rodeo Drive and felt complete awe of your courage. I wished I could temper it with a little timidity, actually, but I never could. Devon, I know you're strong enough."

"Then what exactly is the problem?"

"Devon, you're making a decision based on what happened last night. On a red-hot fire, burning close to the surface. I can give you passion, I can give you the kind of fire that you just keep heaping wood on until it burns bright and fast and explosively . . . and then goes out.

"But you aren't going to be happy with that for long. Your kind of fire runs deep and demands more. It burns soft, and its embers give off a gentle glow. It has to be tended. Cherished. Looked after. Stoked tenderly and patiently."

He looked at her for a long time before he spoke again, his voice rough. "Having you and having to let you go would be worse than never having had you."

"But you already have," she reminded him smoothly.

"Devon, don't make this so hard. I'm trying to tell you I can't give you the things I think you deserve. Security. Steadiness. Presence. You deserve a marriage. And a marriage means a man who can be home on time for supper, and who's going to keep you warm at night, and who will be holding your hand when your children are born, not running around like some middle-aged Rambo in the middle of some nameless jungle somewhere."

"Any chance you're going to give up being a middle-aged Rambo?" she asked softly.

He let out a long breath, and the pain filled his eyes. "No, Devon. It's what I do. It's the only thing I've ever done that made me feel so satisfied inside. I don't expect you to understand this, but I feel as if I change the world in some small way. That good wins out against evil every now and then. And I need that feeling. It's a part of me. If I did something else I couldn't be a man you loved any more."

She smiled at him. "I think I figured that out already. So I'll take you just the way you are."

"Devon, you're riding on a sexual high, and I'm not going to take advantage of that."

"I bet you will," she informed him huskily with a wicked glitter in her eye. She sobered. "Grey, it's for better or worse. I know exactly what I'm getting into. I know you're not going to be home with your slippers and pipe. I know I won't always wake up with you beside me. I know there will be times when you won't be able to tell me what you're doing, times when I won't even know where you are. I know that there are times that you flirt with life and death. I know there will be times when I'll hate your job with a helpless fury.

"But for me it became very clear this afternoon that there's something even scarier than the possibility of your getting hurt on the job, and that's the possibility of my not being there when it happens. Of hearing it on the news five or ten years from now, and knowing I could have had five or ten or twenty or fifty years, and I didn't. The scariest thing isn't what will happen to you. It's what will happen to me if I walk away from the challenge of loving you.

"What will I become? What mockery of the full person that I was meant to be? I'd be out there somewhere, half alive, having refused the challenge of loving, having picked safety over passion. Then I could be one of those people who move in automation through their lives, never feeling pain, but also never seeing colors, never smelling flowers, never laughing to the bottom of their bellies. Is that what you would wish for me, Grey?"

A light came on inside him. The light of someone who had dared not even hope, had thought the dream too bold, the mountains too high. Someone who had resigned himself to not ever having some of the things he wanted most, never being able to scale some chosen peak, only to find himself sitting on that very pinnacle, looking out over crystal skies and lush valleys, being offered the entire world.

A slow smile spread through the weariness of his eyes. "Are you proposing to me, Devon?"

She laughed, undaunted by his no-nonsense tone of voice. He loved her. She could see it dancing in his eyes, a secret let out. That hint of barrenness that had always lurked in his eyes like a lonely sentinel was washed from him. It was like watching the sun warming thick brooding clouds from behind and then, suddenly, piercing them with a blinding burst of silver. She trusted his love for her.

"So I am. And I want you to know I've made one heck of a compromise. I always thought I'd marry a man who liked horses."

A laugh shook his shoulders, but he wouldn't let the sound out. "Devon, no. You don't——"

She leaned close to him. "Grey, just answer for yourself. Just tell me what you want to do. Without taking care of me. Without looking out for me. Without thinking of me and for me. Just tell me what you would do if you were a completely selfish man. If you were free to do anything in the whole world without having to ever worry about the consequences."

He stared at her, and the weariness in his gray eyes was completely replaced by a heart-wrenching wistfulness. "I'd marry you," he whispered. "If I could have anything in the world, I would have you for my wife." He closed his eyes. "And we would have children—three of them. And a house, and two dogs, and a cat. I could probably even handle a pony.''

There was a raw pain whispering through his voice, as if he were a poor man dreaming dreams of impossible riches.

"Deal," she said softly.

"Devon." Her name came off his lips sternly, as if he sought to bring her back to reality. But he could not keep the faint note of hope from her.

"Just kiss me," she commanded.

"Dammit, who's supposed to be the servant here?"

Devon lowered her eyes humbly. "A thousand pardons. Your wish is my command, master."

"Just kiss me," Grey growled his surrender. His raw need was in his voice. "Just kiss me as though you'll never stop."

"Yes, sir," she responded throatily. "Kiss the man, and never stop."

"And don't even pretend that I've got the upper hand."

She giggled. "Grey Carmichael, I knew the first time I slid down the balcony at Redwoods that if I ever, ever let you get the upper hand I would be lost."

"Well, you succeeded," he growled. "I never once felt I had the upper hand."

"Is that right?" she answered softly. "Then why am I lost, anyway? Totally, hopelessly lost?"

"Let's be lost together," he suggested, and his lips took hers. His naked desire was in his kiss and she answered it, opening her mouth to the probing spear of his tongue, feeling the breathtaking tingle of welcome in the core of her being.

He claimed her lips first, and then her mouth, and eyes and ears, and then her neck. His mouth swooped

lower and lower, branding every inch of her, leading
her further and further into the lost valley of rainbow
hues, crystal-sharp air, crashing waves, unleashed
passion.

And then, afraid she was just taking, afraid she
might leave him behind, she turned his attentions back
on him, and led him, her soul mate, down the same
path he had just gone with her. Finally, utterly
breathless with need and love, they entered the mys-
tical glade. Here they were returned to innocence,
where they could explore without any sense of shame
or even time. Time stopped as they worshiped each
other, tasted each other, touched each other, gloried
in the scents of each other. The secrets of each other.
And finally, finally, they loved each other.

A long time later, his arm circled the soft swell of
her naked shoulders. She noticed with fuzzy surprise
that at some point they had made it into the bedroom.
Grey sat with his back braced against the headboard
of his bed. Her head rested contentedly on the broad
plane of his chest, and they both gazed at nothing,
feeling as though they saw for the first time.

"You know," he said, after a long time, his voice
rough with emotion, "I feel as if I've been walking
this long road. It's bleak and dark and cold and
lonely—God, so lonely! And suddenly I've glimpsed
the end of it. A light burning, promising warmth and
comfort. I've been heading home for a long, long
time, every single event of my life conspiring to bring
me to the moment when I would recognize that that
light that burned in your eyes was where I could lay
my weary hurting heart down, to rest, to be healed."

"Me, too," she whispered. "Mine has been a different kind of loneliness. The loneliness a person feels

when they're imprisoned by their own roles, when they can't be real for people. The road's been long and lonely for me too. And that's all I'll ever ask of you. That when we're together, the loneliness won't be there. For those precious moments, that the loneliness won't be there.''

He kissed her again, with tenderness this time, instead of passion, with his gray eyes insatiable on her face, beholding her with wonder. In his eyes, in the openness of the affection she saw there, she knew another truth, and tucked it in her heart like a small gem.

Grey didn't even have to be here beside her—not all the time. His love would stay with her, even when he was gone. And hers would also warm him when he was away, and their loneliness was behind them now.

''That's what made it so incredibly hard with Alfonso this afternoon,'' he murmured. ''God, if there was a man alive who could understand the desperation of loving you without hope, it was me. Who could understand the hell of looking at you without being able to touch you, of talking to you, without being able to dream of a future with you...'' His voice drifted away, pained.

''I thought about him this afternoon,'' she told him, ''and felt such grief and guilt that I'd been so insensitive as to not even notice——''

''You couldn't have done anything different, Devon,'' he told her sharply.

''I know. I didn't have the tools or the experience, but next time——''

''Next time?'' Grey practically yelled.

She giggled, despite herself. "I just mean I'd probably know if a man ever fell in love with me again, and wouldn't treat his affection with such a cavalier lack of interest."

"And what exactly would you do?" Grey asked tightly.

"I'd tell him I was married and madly in love with my husband before his fantasy became too serious." She batted her lashes at him innocently. "I will be, won't I?"

"You'll be safely married as soon as the law... and your father... allow it," he growled.

"Oh, yes," she said, wrinkling her nose, "Father. Do you think we could just——"

"Absolutely not, Devon. I'm going to be old-fashioned enough to ask your father for your hand. You know that, don't you?"

"I suspected."

"Um. But not old-fashioned enough to listen if he says no."

"He won't say no," she said. "That wasn't my worry. Good grief! This is his dream come true."

"Are you kidding? Your father? I would have thought a multimillionaire more in keeping with his ambition."

"Can you think of one other way I'd ever have agreed to have all those security people at my wedding? What other way could he possibly get a permanent bodyguard into my life?"

Grey laughed—a good sound, free and easy.

"My concern is that he'll want something large," she went on. "White gowns and morning suits——"

"*Morning suits?*" Grey echoed, his tone slightly strangled.

Devon was pleased by the sound. "It'll take weeks, of course—longer, maybe. And I'd never see you. Fittings, invitations, showers..."

"We'll make a run up to Nevada tomorrow and get married," he said decisively.

She smiled a satisfied smile, and tried to hide it, but not quickly enough.

"You sneaky little witch," he said with mock chagrin. "You can't wait, can you?"

She blushed scarlet, but held her ground. "No."

He laughed, a deeply appreciative sound. "I love your desire, Devon. That nearly hidden candle that flickers within you, that a man catches sight of every now and then like a light burning in a cabin window, far away through the driven snow. No wonder you drive men to near madness!"

He noted her changed expression, and said softly, "I'm sorry, Devon, I didn't mean that the way it came out. I wasn't referring to Alfonso. I wasn't even thinking about him."

"What will happen to him?" she asked softly.

"I found him a good lawyer, Devon, an old friend from the Marines who does me a favor every now and then. He'll be going for a psychiatric evaluation before anything else. Everything will be fine, Devon, believe me."

"I do," she whispered.

He smiled tenderly. "Save that one for tomorrow."

"Grey, could you kiss me again?"

"My God, you're insatiable! What am I going to do with all this newfound desire of yours?"

"Rise to the challenge," she murmured in his ear, "for the next forty or fifty years."

"Don't think small, Devon," he chided her, his tone teasing, but his eyes full of love as he gazed at her. "For eternity."

"For eternity," she agreed in a husky whisper.

THREE UNFORGETTABLE HEROINES
THREE AWARD-WINNING AUTHORS

Untamed
MAVERICK HEARTS

A unique collection of historical short stories that capture the spirit of America's last frontier.

HEATHER GRAHAM POZZESSERE—over 10 million copies of her books in print worldwide
Lonesome Rider—The story of an Eastern widow and the renegade half-breed who becomes her protector.

PATRICIA POTTER—an author whose books are consistently Waldenbooks bestsellers
Against the Wind—Two people, battered by heartache, prove that love can heal all.

JOAN JOHNSTON—award-winning Western historical author with 17 books to her credit
One Simple Wish—A woman with a past discovers that dreams really do come true.

Join us for an exciting journey West with
UNTAMED
Available in July, wherever Harlequin books are sold.

**Harlequin is proud to present our
best authors and their best books.
Always the best for your reading
pleasure!**

Throughout 1993, Harlequin will bring you
exciting books by some of the top names in
contemporary romance!

In July
look for
The Ties That Bind by

Shannon wanted him seven days a week....

Dark, compelling, mysterious Garth Sheridan was no
mere boy next door—even if he did rent the cottage
beside Shannon Raine's.

She was intrigued by the hard-nosed exec, but for
Shannon it was all or nothing. Either break the
undeniable bonds between them . . . or tear down the
barriers surrounding Garth and discover the truth.

Don't miss THE TIES THAT BIND . . .
wherever Harlequin books are sold.

Fifty red-blooded, white-hot, true-blue hunks from every State in the Union!

Beginning in May, look for MEN MADE IN AMERICA! Written by some of our most popular authors, these stories feature fifty of the strongest, sexiest men, each from a different state in the union!

Two titles available every other month at your favorite retail outlet.

In July, look for:

CALL IT DESTINY by Jayne Ann Krentz (Arizona)
ANOTHER KIND OF LOVE by Mary Lynn Baxter (Arkansas)

In September, look for:

DECEPTIONS by Annette Broadrick (California)
STORMWALKER by Dallas Schulze (Colorado)

You won't be able to resist MEN MADE IN AMERICA!